ALSO BY MARK LINDQUIST

Never Mind Nirvana

Carnival Desires

Sad Movies

MARK LINDQUIST

The King of Methlehem

A NOVEL

Simon & Schuster

New York   London   Toronto   Sydney

SIMON & SCHUSTER
Rockefeller Center
1230 Avenue of the Americas
New York, NY 10020

SIMON & SCHUSTER and colophon are registered trademarks of Simon & Schuster, Inc.

For information about special discounts for bulk purchases, please contact Simon & Schuster Special Sales at 1-800-456-6798 or business@simonandschuster.com.

Book design by Ellen R. Sasahara

Manufactured in the United States of America

10 9 8 7 6 5 4 3 2 1

Library of Congress Cataloging-in-Publication Data

Lindquist, Mark, 1959–
    The King of Methlehem / by Mark Lindquist.
        p. cm.
    1. Detectives—Washington (State)—Tacoma—Fiction. 2. Drug traffic—Fiction. 3. Methamphetamine abuse—Fiction. 4. Tacoma (Wash.)—Fiction. I. Title.

PS3562.I51165K56   2007
813'.54—dc22   2006037311

ISBN-13: 978-1-4165-3577-5
ISBN-10:   1-4165-3577-2

for chelsea

You never know what is enough until you know what is more than enough.

—William Blake, *Marriage of Heaven and Hell*

tweeker 1. A methamphetamine user. Tweekers are known for their extreme paranoia, flagrant dishonesty, and lack of non-tweeker friends. A tweeker will steal your stuff and then help you look for it.

If you let those goddamned tweekers come to your party, don't expect to have your stereo in the morning.

From www.urbandictionary.com

HAD TO TELL YOU LIES

I had to tell you lies to help you get to the truth.

This is the motto of Detective Wyatt James, who believes a good old-fashioned dialogue is the surest way to solve anything, though sometimes the specter of coercion is necessary to keep the conversation lively.

"Let's hear it, Marvin," he says.

"Hear what?"

Marvin squirms and adjusts the cuffs on his wrists, aggravated by the cold steel rubbing against his scabbed skin. Over long johns he wears shredded Levi's and a gray T-shirt that reads: REHAB IS FOR QUITTERS.

"Don't waste my time," Wyatt says, walking in a circle around the scrawny tweeker.

"I don't know what you want, I swear."

Sweat drips from Marvin's pocked forehead. He licks his teeth, dying brown and gray pegs poking out from swollen gums. Judging by the dental deterioration, Wyatt figures Marvin has been using for at least three years.

Though a plainclothes detective, Wyatt wears a uniform of a kind: khakis, a button-down oxford shirt, and a worn blue blazer. He looks like an overgrown college kid except for the Glock .40 on his hip next to his badge. His parents named him Wyatt after the Peter Fonda character in *Easy Rider* and, weirdly, Wyatt grew up with a vague physical resemblance to the lanky movie star.

"Have I been fucking with you, Marvin?" Wyatt asks, stopping in front of him.

"No, I guess not."

"You *guess* not?"

"No, you haven't."

"Then why are you fucking with me?"

"I'm not," Marvin says, glancing at him, then looking back down. "I swear to God."

The more they swear to God, the more they're lying.

Wyatt could conduct this interview back at the station, but he prefers the eerie atmosphere of the cook site. They are in a clearing surrounded by fir trees. On a grill mounted on rocks over a campfire is a shallow pie pan crusted with white powder and littered around the site are mason jars, porn magazines, shredded lithium batteries, cans of muriatic acid, a propane tank with blue tinting around the valve, and a plastic soda bottle with rubber tubing snaking out to nowhere.

Despite a chilly fall breeze, ammonia lingers in the air and stings Wyatt's nostrils. He is considering his next move when the wind suddenly picks up and the tree branches rustle.

Seemingly out of nowhere a dirty white Starbucks paper cup rolls toward Wyatt's feet and stops with the black and white mermaid inside the green circle facing up.

A sign.

"Howard was here?"

Marvin twitches in a nodlike motion, but Wyatt cannot be sure if this is an answer or a random tweeker jitter.

Wyatt once read about an East Indian monkey trap in which a hollowed-out coconut with rice inside is chained to a peg in the ground. The trap has a hole carved in the coconut and the hole is large enough for a monkey to reach inside and grab the rice, but small enough that the monkey cannot pull his hand back out while holding on to the rice. Even as hunters approach, the monkeys hold fast.

Tweekers remind Wyatt of these monkeys—they typically cannot let go of the rice, no matter the cost.

"Do you want to talk? Or do you want to just go to jail?"

"Talk."

"Then start talking."

"What do you wanna know?"

"The truth."

Marvin dimly weighs his options, the upsides and downsides of snitching flapping around in his meth-damaged brain like bats.

"Was the midget here?" Wyatt tries.

"What?"

Genuine confusion contorts Marvin's face and Wyatt knows he missed. He has heard that Howard sometimes works with a midget, but it could be a joke, the sort of semi-amusing information tweekers occasionally dissemble. Clearly Marvin is not in on the joke, if it is one.

"Who all was here?" Wyatt asks, quickly moving past his misstep.

"Just me and him."

"Just you and Howard?"

"Yeah."

"Tell me what you know."

"Like what?"

"Let's start with what he looks like."

"He's . . . short, I guess."

"How short?"

"Five-foot-six or so."

"Complexion?"

"You know, the usual. Very white."

"Hair?"

"Long, dark blond."

"Facial hair?"

"Just kinda unshaved. And a goatee."

"Age?"

"Around thirty. Maybe forty."

Wyatt looks at him, not pleased with this answer.

"I don't know," Marvin insists, convincingly. "It's hard to tell sometimes."

"Tats?"

"I don't remember."

"Anything else about him you do remember?"

"Well, he always wears black cowboy boots."

"Good. Anything else?"

"That's . . . it."

"What about his real name?"

"I don't know his real name. Nobody does. I swear."

"How about his mom? Does his mom know his name?"

This flummoxes Marvin.

Patience is key to questioning a suspect, but Wyatt does not have much of that these days. He attributes this to his assignment to the meth lab team, which he mistakenly thought would be a low-stress break from homicides but instead has been a grim tour through doom and decay.

"Quit fucking with me, Marvin."

"I'm not, I swear."

Waiting for Marvin to crack, allowing time for meth paranoia to build as Marvin continues to come down, Wyatt steps around the site. He kicks the Starbucks cup, stops at a boom box on the ground, leans over, clicks it on.

"Ain't found a way to kill me yet . . ."

Alice in Chains from the *MTV Unplugged* recording, which Wyatt also owns.

"I went to high school with Jerry Cantrell," Marvin says. "Spanaway Lake. Not far from here."

"Yeah," Wyatt says, turning off the CD. "I know where Cantrell went to high school."

"He was in choir," Marvin adds.

"Do I seem like I give a crap about Jerry Cantrell right now?"

"No," Marvin says, shaking his head.

"If you don't fuck with me, I won't fuck with you. But if you *do* fuck with me . . ."

Though Wyatt has never beat a suspect, it happens so often and gratuitously on television and in the movies that he figures the scare factor can work for him. He steps directly in front of Marvin and puts his hand behind his back and slouches and tilts his head, mirroring Marvin's posture, a standard technique for establishing rapport.

"What kind of criminal history do you have, Marvin?"

"Just misdemeanors. No felony convictions yet."

"*Yet.* Well, I guess it's good to leave yourself something to work toward."

Wyatt smiles, and then so does Marvin, lopsided and snaggle-toothed.

"There are some advantages to being a nobody, Marvin. Namely, we don't care about you. We don't care if you go to prison or walk. You get what I'm saying?"

Marvin nods. Wyatt nods along with him, encouraging him in the direction he is leaning, *pull your hand out of the coconut.*

"So where can I find him?"

Marvin's eyes blink and dart rapidly, as skittish as the brain behind them, avoiding Wyatt's gaze. Raindrops start falling, pinging on pans and the blue tarp.

"Time's running out, Marvin."

"He won't find out I told?"

"This is confidential background, just between us."

I had to tell you lies to help you get to the truth.

"And if I tell you?"

"Truth is its own reward."

Though Marvin suspects Wyatt is hustling him, even mocking him, he decides it does not matter.

Nothing matters, except staying free.

With freakish focus Howard methodically pops Sudafed pills from blister packages into a blender, *pop, pop, pop,* his filthy fingers trembling with anticipation like a poker player with the winning hand. His eyes are red, pupils dilated, skin pale, blond hair long and stringy and dirty.

Piling up behind him on the floor of the kitchen area of the double-wide trailer are dozens of crumpled blister packs. In the corner sits Amber, a skinny tweeker transfixed in front of a television. She is doing exactly what Howard told her to do—staring at a black and white image of an empty rural road, looking for signs of trouble in the dim light of dusk. Howard, who prides himself on superior security precautions, wired the television to a camera he set up on a post at the end of the dirt and gravel driveway.

Amber's four-year-old girl sits nearby on the floor in a purple jumper, eating potato chips and playing with the bag, mesmerized by the crinkling sound. She occasionally glances up at the television or the adults.

"Mom?"

"Sssshhh."

Rain patters lightly on the aluminum roof. Howard cooks regularly at Amber's trailer, which is parked on the property of a couple in their seventies who allow Amber to keep her trailer on the three-acre rural lot because they know her mother, who works as a waitress at a Sizzler in Puyallup. The couple is clueless, oblivious to the occasional chemical odors and the poisonous meth waste Howard has been dumping onto their land.

As soon as Howard pops the last of the blister packs, he turns the three-speed blender on high. The pills disintegrate into powder and the blender pitcher fills with a cloud of white dust.

He feels a Pavlovian rush as the process begins.

Two mason jars with coffee filters set in the mouths are ready on the kitchen counter. He pours the powder in the filters, then adds HEET, America's "#1 selling brand of gas-line antifreeze," through the powder. This filters out the binder from the pseudo pills.

He pours the pasty mess from the mason jars into a twelve-inch frying pan set on simmer, which evaporates the methanol and leaves purified pseudo powder in the pan.

"How's it going?" Amber asks, hand tapping her thigh.

"Shut up. Watch the monitor."

When Howard started cooking a few years ago, he burned out a friend's trailer, and then a shed, and then a motel room, and then his girlfriend's apartment. He subsequently refined his technique.

He uses the so-called Nazi method of production because it is the easiest and quickest: extraction, reaction, and gassing. Contrary to tweeker lore, the modern Nazi technique was not developed by Nazis or even used in the Third Reich.

Though the Nazis did feed their World War II troops uppers that included methamphetamine, as did the Japanese and the Allies, the labs of that era were designed for mass production and employed a process far more complicated than the one practiced in mobile homes and kitchens across contemporary America.

The currently popular Nazi method was developed in the 1980s by a chemistry student at a Midwest university who discovered that the Birch reduction method could be used to reduce pseudoephedrine to methamphetamine, and *presto, meth-making for dummies.*

This ambitious student wrote the recipe on a sheet of notebook paper, which was copied repeatedly and passed around like a salacious rumor. Because the original paper happened to have Nazi swastika doodling in the margins, the technique became known as the Nazi method.

The first Nazi lab was busted in California in 1988. Seven years later local police found the first Nazi meth lab site in Pierce County, Washington, though they did not initially realize they had stumbled onto a trend. The cook reportedly taught countless other locals his process and it spread with amazing rapidity because it was simple and all the ingredients were legal and easily available.

Though pseudoephedrine is becoming increasingly difficult to obtain in volume, Howard believes the Nazi method produces the best product. After he has completed the first stage, the extraction of pseudo from the pseudoephedrine, he straps on latex gloves and a white disposable dust mask over his mouth and nose with the theatricality of a mad scientist. He is ready for the reaction stage.

Next to the oatmeal on a kitchen shelf is a jar with lithium strips stored in kerosene, which Amber helped extract from Eveready batteries earlier. Howard, like most tweekers, prefers Eveready because of the Energizer Bunny ads, which he and other tweekers believe to be an inside meth joke. He adds the lithium into the frying pan.

He opens the propane tank and pumps anhydrous ammonia over the pseudo and the lithium. Vapors rise toward his unprotected eyes. He stirs with a spatula, turning the sludge blue and gray. To expedite the evaporation of the ammonia he heats the pan up a touch further, adding water to quench the reaction.

"Mommy, what's that smell?"

"Shut up."

"It's not nice to say shut up."

Continuing to add water, Howard stirs until the concoction turns cloudy white. According to tweeker lore, a penny should be added at this stage, but Howard researched this on the Internet and could not find any justification in chemistry for this, so he assumes it is like throwing a coin into a fountain, *superstitious and futile.*

Into a mason jar Howard pours the paste from the frying pan. Next he adds toluene. Ether is cleaner and more efficient, but Howard passed out the only time he used ether and woke up with a hangover and a burned hand.

He pulls the jar close to his face and stares as a bilayered liquid forms—*molecules of meth*—and he nods along, *"Yesssss."* He only has one stage to go and he is shaking. He sets down the jar and picks up a turkey baster and begins sucking up the top layer and squirting it into another mason jar.

This is methamphetamine oil, but not yet methamphetamine hydrochloride, *the real stuff that makes you get naked and climb the tree.*

"You stay," he says to Amber, lowering his mask and passing her a walkie-talkie that is the companion to the one on his hip.

"Cook safe, Howard."

"Shut up, don't call me H-o-w-a-r-d in front of the k-i-fucking-d."

"Who's she gonna t-e-l?"

"Why must I live my life surrounded by morons?" he mutters, then picks up the jar containing the siphoned-off oil and carries it outside toward the ramshackle wooden toolshed, which glows blue from a Coleman lamp he left on earlier. He walks quickly through the dark, hunched over to shield the mouth of the jar from the rain.

Howard has thirteen aliases, all backed up by Washington State driver's licenses. Howard A. Schultz is his current and favorite identity. He paid one of his runners two grams for the date of birth, address, and Social Security number of the Starbucks coffee mogul.

He sometimes worries that he has stuck with this moniker too long. He enjoys being well known—he craves the underground fame, is proud of his place in tweeker lore—but he also recognizes the hazards of being the top cook in Pierce County or, as Howard likes to call the county that leads the western United States in methamphetamine production, *Methlehem* County.

If you want to make movies, you go to Hollywood. If you want to play poker professionally, you go to Las Vegas. And if you want to be the meth king, you go to Pierce County, Washington, Howard is fond of proclaiming. He grew up in Woodinville, a town north of Seattle, but after his first stay in prison, a short one for burglary, he was released to a halfway house in Tacoma, which proved to be an excellent networking opportunity. He quickly befriended addicts and cooks from around the county and recognized the "high-growth" market for methamphetamine.

Entering the shed, he sets the meth oil down on top of a broken freezer that serves as a storage container. Stocked alongside the tools on rickety shelves is muriatic acid, aluminum foil, a Dr Pepper bottle, rubber tubing, and gaffer's tape—everything he needs to create an HCL generator for the gassing stage.

Under the spooky glow of the lamp hanging from the low roof, he mixes muriatic acid and balls of aluminum foil in the Dr Pepper bottle. Usually he uses rock salt and drain opener, which makes for a cleaner and whiter final product, but Amber used up the drain opener on *a goddamned clogged drain,* so Howard must improvise.

He pokes a tube into the plastic bottle, wraps gaffer's tape around the opening, and the gas generated by the acid and foil, hydrogen chloride, bubbles through the hose and into the methamphetamine oil.

"Time to snow," he whispers, kneeling ceremoniously.

Sparkles form in the haze as the methamphetamine crystals begin forming—white and dirty beige—clouding the mason jar like a snowstorm.

Because the muriatic acid dirties up the product with tan patches, he will have to clean it with acetone before putting it on the market.

Ice, crank, speed, zoom, it all means money.

Howard gets high just watching this, the tingle spiking through his body. He is reminded of snow globes he shook incessantly as an ADHD child. Enraptured, he does not hear the walkie-talkie at the first crackle.

"Howard," Amber repeats.

He is about to tell her not to call him that, not to call him at all unless it is an absolute emergency, *don't bother me, I'm working,* when the walkie-talkie crackles again.

"Howard, cops!"

"You sure this is the right damn place?" Wyatt asks, stopping the gray Ford Taurus with its low nose pointed up the narrow muddy driveway surrounded by blackberry bushes.

"Pretty sure," Marvin says from the back seat.

"*Pretty* sure?"

"Sorry, every goddamn road out here looks the same. Doesn't it? Don't you think?" Marvin's shaking and babbling. "But this is it. I'm pretty sure. We're like out between Bonney Lake and Sumner, sort of?"

"We're where you told me to go."

"Okay, well, a trailer should be at the top of the driveway."

Headlights shine into the streaky drizzle and darkness as they bounce up the driveway, and then Wyatt clicks on the high beams and there's the trailer, an old silver double-wide with a blue tarp hanging off one end.

Trailer, blue tarp, looks like a meth lab.

Leaving Marvin locked in the back seat, engine running, headlights on, Wyatt steps out and walks up to the front door. His senses are attuned to his surroundings as the drizzle falls quietly. He can hear scurrying inside, the micelike noises he usually hears when tweekers are home.

"Hello," Amber says, opening the front door about six inches, just enough so the child can look out past Amber's skinny thighs.

Immediately Wyatt can smell the ammonia. "Hello, ma'am. I'm Detective Wyatt James." He smiles amiably as he opens his blue blazer enough to display his badge and gun. "Is anyone else inside?"

"Just my child," Amber says, switching unconsciously into a pathetic whine.

"You mind if I come in out of the rain and talk to you?" he says. "You have the right to say no," he adds, "but I'd like to come in if I could." Police officers must, under the law, inform residents they can refuse them entry, but experienced criminals already know this, so it is only the amateurs who allow police inside without a warrant. "I'd like to talk to you about someone," Wyatt says casually, "if you don't mind."

Amber has been in jail before and does not want to return and, in her experience, pissing off police officers often results in a trip downtown, while giving information can lead to a free pass.

"Okay."

"Thanks," Wyatt says. From his inside pocket he pulls out a "Ferrier warnings" form, which reiterates that Amber has the right to refuse him entry, limit his search, or revoke her consent at any time, and he has her sign the sheet acknowledging these rights, *blah, blah, blah*.

As he steps inside, blister packs crush under his shoes. He scans the filthy interior and amid the sundry trash he picks out the blender, the coffee filters, the propane tank, mason jars, porn magazines, and a black cylindrical object that could be either a butt plug or a chew toy.

And this is after *she had time to clean up.*

"How long ago did he leave?"

"Who?"

"Howard."

"Howard?"

Amber fumbles long enough for Wyatt to know that Marvin gave them good intel, albeit too late.

"Yes, *Howard.*"

"Howard," she repeats again, jittery and on the down slide. Wyatt figures she was left without any product, a hasty exit, no doubt.

"Howard Schultz," he says impatiently, eyes watering from the ammonia remnants. "The cook." He puts his palm over the frying pan with white crust, *still warm.* "Where did he go?"

"He left."

"Yes, we've established that. Where did he go?"

"I don't know."

Amber's child is on the floor watching the road and driveway on the television monitor. Wyatt studies the screen for a moment, realizes that his approach was observed. "Let's get out of here," he says when his throat starts to itch. "Your child, too."

Wyatt herds them outside. A cat scampers out with them, disappearing quickly. Between the trailer and his car, Wyatt steps in front of Amber and her child so that he is backlit, partially blocking out the glare of the headlamps. Mist has replaced the drizzle.

"So what's your name?" he asks.

"Amber."

"Of course. Last name?"

After a long pause she says, "Johnson."

Wyatt assumes this as a lie but is not inclined to bother with calling her on it yet.

"Were you helping him cook?"

"Who?"

"Or did he do all the cooking and promise you some product in exchange?"

"That."

"What?"

"He promised me some."

Always works: give them two choices and they will pick what they think is the lesser crime.

"So you let him use your place to cook meth?"

"Yeah."

"Okay. Where did he go?"

"I don't know."

"You don't know if you're going to tell me?"

"I don't know."

"How much do you know about him?"

"Nothing. I just met him today, at this party, at this, like, apartment, more like a motel. . . ."

She's so obviously lying, so obviously tweaking, so obviously useless, Wyatt cuts her off by holding a hand up like a traffic cop. Sometimes he just cannot take another damn lie.

"Stop."

"No, no, I swear—"

"Stop."

"Okay, okay."

Wyatt looks down at the child standing behind Amber's legs. His own eyes are still watering, but she stares back at him with clear pupils, apparently immune to the ammonia. He expects meth will show up in her urine test from secondhand smoke and dermal exposure.

"Have you had dinner?" he asks the child, bending down, hands on knees.

She shakes her head.

"You hungry?"

She nods.

"There's a Denny's down the road. Have you been there?"

She nods, almost smiles.

"We're going to meet a nice woman from the government there, and you can get something to eat, okay?"

The child nods agreeably, either uncomprehending or unfazed.

Flipping open his cell phone, Wyatt rings the on-duty supervisor and gives him a situation update and asks for Child Protective Services and the meth lab team.

"You're calling in CPS?" Amber says when he's finished with the call. "Why?"

"Because you're going downtown."

"To jail?"

He reads Amber her Miranda rights by memory and the child mouths along, as though to a nursery rhyme she has heard many times before.

"Tell Grandma I need bail money," Amber says.

"Turn around." Wyatt clicks on the cuffs. "If you decide you want to talk about Howard, let me know." He turns her around by her shoulders and slides his card in the front pocket of her jeans. She is not ready to pull her hand out of the coconut yet, but tweekers generally detox after about twelve weeks. "I'm Detective Wyatt James. Your public defender will know who I am."

I am, I am Superman, and I know what's happening.... This snippet of a song lyric plays over and over in Howard's head as he runs for what seems like miles, tromping in his black cowboy boots, through the woods, across grassy fields, over wooden fences, until he arrives at an intersection, where he stops to finally catch his ragged breath. He sounds like Darth Vader.

To the outside eye Howard looks depleted and decrepit, wheezing like a man dying from the plague, but inside he feels dynamic and destined for greatness, ruling the world like a man holding the hammer of the gods. As dopamine surges through his brain cells he is proud that he is zooming on his own homemade fuel, euphoric that he is wildly free, confident that he can outsmart the cops every time, and these sensations flood together in a kaleidoscope of sweaty, teeth-grinding, finger-twitching, head-bobbing, crazy ecstasy.

I am, I am Superman....

Above him a nearly full moon emerges between dark clouds. He steps into the shadows behind the stop sign, clumsily sits in the tall and wet grass. The closest streetlight is a hundred yards away and there are no cars coming. He pulls out a cell phone, calls a taxi service.

Despite all his licenses, Howard does not drive. He does not own anything that can be traced back to him. The cell phone is registered to Ted Nugent, with a PO box in University Place. When the wireless company eventually shuts down the service for lack of payment, as they invariably do, he will get another phone with one of his other identities.

He collects SSI, Social Security Insurance payments, because he is "disabled" and "unable to maintain employment" after his stroke-resembling collapse in the county jail that followed a week-long meth binge. The disability payments are enough for him to live on even when he is not supplementing his income with meth sales. He relies on the kindness of tweekers for shelter and his only expenses are for manufacturing supplies, Kools, taxis, alcohol, and fast food.

I am, I am Superman. . . .

This song keeps playing in his brain, and he does not know it is an R.E.M. song and if he did he would be amused by the band's name.

When the cab approaches, Howard stands up and waves it down, trying to appear normal and amiable, but he is grinning and fidgeting like a fiend.

Still, the cabbie stops. Howard gives directions to Brandy's house on the outskirts of Eatonville. Amber was fun, but Howard was tired of her squalid little trailer and mouthy four-year-old child. "Bag 'ho" is his phrase for addicts like Amber, women who will have sex for whatever meth residue is left at the bottom of a baggie.

Brandy actually owns a house, not a trailer. She inherited it from her parents when they died. Though she used to share it with her white supremacist boyfriend, word on the street is that he went to prison for domestic violence. Howard stayed with Brandy for a few weeks before she hooked up with the wife-beater and he expects her door is always open for him.

Though he thinks she has sad eyes, which he calls cow eyes, Brandy can be attractive sometimes. Better yet, she has a daughter she saddled with the name Porsche who wore hip huggers and chokers at eleven and *must be twelve by now.*

I am, I am Superman, and I can do anything. . . .

Tacoma is famous for its crime.

Serial killer and rapist Ted Bundy lived in Tacoma, as did serial killer and rapist Robert Yates. Gary Ridgeway, the Green River Killer, is said to have buried bodies in Pierce County. Serial child rapist and murderer Joseph Edward Duncan is from Tacoma. John Lee Malvo and John Allen Muhammad, the D.C. snipers, used a Bushmaster rifle from Bull's Eye Shooter Supply in their former hometown of Tacoma.

David Brame, the Tacoma police chief, murdered his wife and shot himself in a Pierce County strip mall parking lot in 2003. This seemed like a high point, or a low point, until two years later when a disgruntled twenty-year-old meth user carried two semi-automatic weapons to the Tacoma Mall and cut down seven shoppers, prompting Charles Mudede, a reporter with *The Stranger,* a Seattle alternative weekly, to write, "The only time Tacoma makes national news is when one of its citizens opens fire on innocent people."

Mr. Mudede is not entirely correct. Tacoma and Pierce County also make national news for leading the country in methamphetamine labs, and it was national news in 2004 when Sperling's Best Places, a research firm, rated Tacoma "America's Most Stressed-Out City," topping such high-tension contenders as Miami, New Orleans, and New York, and it was national news in 2005 when Stacy Fuson, a *Playboy* Playmate and Tacoma native, became the St. Pauli beer girl. Celebrated in the local *News Tribune* as a Tacoma girl "through and through," she moved to Los Angeles.

Downtown, in the most stressed-out city in the country, is quiet at nine o'clock on a Tuesday, when Wyatt exits the freeway. He returns his unmarked squad car to the parking lot of the County-City Building, a plain eleven-story box containing courtrooms, the County Council chambers, the sheriff's department, and the cramped offices of the Pierce County Prosecuting Attorney.

This classically drab example of functional fifties architecture replaced an ominous gothic courthouse, and Wyatt continually laments the lack of grandeur and gravitas the larger replacement presents to its visitors.

Wyatt could drive the county car to his apartment, but he lives less than a mile away and parking is difficult there and he likes the exercise of walking and the meditative aspect as well. He needs wind-down time before he can sleep.

Though it is not raining, he removes a black umbrella from the trunk. The trek ahead is only about twenty minutes, but he does not want to bet on the rain letting up for long. A light wind blows from the north and the horizon is dark.

He walks briskly south on Tacoma Avenue, stepping through the fallen leaves from the Flowering Cherry trees, enjoying the crisp fall air. Earlier in the day the sidewalk was filled with animal rights protesters passing out leaflets demanding the death penalty for a defendant who poisoned a dog. Child molesters, rapists, and murderers are on trial every day and nobody seems to notice, but when an animal suffers, outrage follows.

At the corner of Eleventh and Tacoma Avenue, Wyatt takes a left, enjoys the postcard view of the steel girders of the Murray Morgan Bridge lit up ahead. On his right are office fronts for bail-bonding companies, the dominant business around the County-City Building, and tweeker alley, a dead-end street near a homeless shelter where riffraff gather to do drugs, make connections, urinate and defecate, and generally keep the area off-limits to anyone but criminals and police.

Overlooking tweeker alley is the wooden deck of a new nightclub, Syren, trying to make a go of it where many have failed. In the summer hipsters congregate near the railing, smoking cigarettes and drinking microbrews while observing the peccancy below. Tonight there is only one couple outside and they are staring out across the alley as if it does not exist.

Wyatt figures he could, if he wanted to take a stroll, observe half a dozen crimes without even trying. The city has conceded tweeker alley to the ne'er-do-wells. Wyatt sometimes wonders why the homeless folks dragging ratty sleeping bags over their shoulders do not leave the cold and wet Northwest for warm and dry Southern California.

Maybe they, like he, prefer the gloom and the gray?

A couple blocks south of this Wyatt takes a right on Broadway, passing a fountain of concrete blocks and cascading water with an enormous sculpture of pink and tan fiberglass salmon poking out of the water on a metal pipe. *Northwest art: fish and water.* He considers stopping by Fujiya, a sushi restaurant and downtown landmark, but it is closing up on schedule with the other civilized portions of the city.

A block behind him is the Winthrop, a former grand hotel that currently functions as federally subsidized housing for addicts, dealers, and their unfortunate low-income neighbors. Ahead of him, just beyond the Sea Grill, is the new $65 million convention center, lights on as always, an astonishing four-hundred-foot-tall trapezoid, a brightly lit vision of the future with a slanted wall of stainless steel mesh and green-tinted windows looking out over the city toward Commencement Bay.

Just past the convention center he crosses a triangular concrete park toward Pacific Avenue, strolling past five stepped infinity pools that slowly spill into each other. Reflecting off the dark water is the sleek new Tacoma Art Museum, which is constructed with steel and glass much like the convention center, another testament to urban renewal.

He recalls twenty years ago when all of downtown Tacoma was like tweeker alley: prostitutes, drug dealers, bums, and thugs. Customers came from all over the county, including from the two military posts, Fort Lewis and McChord Air Force Base. You would not walk around in soft-soled shoes because of the syringes that popped up more numerous than weeds on an abandoned playground. In some ways it was a cop's dream city: real life that resembled the caricatures of crime meccas in graphic novels.

However, the dotcom wave of prosperity that swept through Tacoma's northern neighbor Seattle flooded into Tacoma as well. Pulp mills, which accounted for the infamous Tacoma aroma, began modernizing or shutting down. In 1993 the transition was symbolically sealed when the Asarco copper smelter tower, one of the city's chief polluters, tumbled in a staged implosion. The Environmental Protection Agency is still appraising the damage to the waterfront.

Tacoma and Seattle, like their California cousin San Francisco, are port towns. Ports are the most vital cities. Ideas, trends, and adventurous spirits drift in by land and sea. Seattle's cool peaked in 1992 when Nirvana became a phenomenon and Microsoft, uninhibited by the Justice Department, was taking over the world.

Coolness, though, like freshness, fades, and as it ebbed from Seattle it flowed into Tacoma. People who would shudder at the thought of crossing the Pierce County border in the 1980s were shopping for Tacoma houses and lofts by the late 1990s. For years the underdog to Seattle, Tacoma emerged in the new millennium as the hip and gritty alternative, humming with possibilities.

"Tacoma is on a roll," Mayor Bill Baarsma continually announces at the rising number of civic events filling local calendars.

Still, the crime continues in this frontier town.

Criminal subcultures took root in the 1970s when the Department of Corrections, which administers the prison system, began dumping hundreds of violent felons, sex offenders, and drug addicts into Pierce County every year through work release and halfway house programs. Pierce County Prosecutor Gerry Horne calls it the crime warp.

Power brokers in Seattle, heavily invested in the state's economic capital and its world-famous image, successfully keep their fair share of felons out of King County. Seattleites find it much easier to be understanding of criminals and their unfortunate childhoods if the crime stays south.

Drawn to underdogs, challenges, and adrenaline, Wyatt moved to Tacoma—or T-Town, as he calls it—when he graduated from law school. He had already decided to be a cop rather than a lawyer. This was done partly because law school bored him nearly to tears, and partly to aggravate his father, but proved to be a fitting choice despite his motives. He does not discuss his law degree with fellow cops, just as he does not discuss his colonoscopy.

Sometimes he wishes he had a more colorful backstory, such as the detective in one of his favorite books who had a hooker mom who was mysteriously murdered because of her scandalous involvement with powerful and corrupt people. Scandal and mystery intrigue Wyatt. The biggest mystery at his own house was when his father broke some china without telling his mother.

Wyatt tried marriage after his first few years on the force. In retrospect, he is not sure what the attraction to his ex-wife was. She was pretty, primarily by virtue of her youth, and he believed their mutual affection, bouncy in the beginning, would evolve into a romantic, mellow, mutually understanding harmony, the two of them chuckling together over the Sunday paper. Instead they became indifferent roommates.

Nearly a year after the relationship died, she initiated a divorce. He surrendered the house, started renting downtown, and soon decided it was a good thing that he had lost the house and the wife. He is forty years old and loves his job and does not mind his age or the detours he took getting here.

The last stretch of his walk home takes him across a corner of the University of Washington Tacoma campus with its meticulously restored brick buildings and well-lit walkways. The shell of a transformer house for the Snoqualmie Falls Power Company still stands, but the interior has been converted to a library and a twenty-foot glass chandelier by Tacoma native Dale Chihuly hangs in the lobby glowing red, putting Wyatt in mind of a giant squid.

Just as sporadic raindrops start to fall, blown by the north wind, he arrives at his building's security door under a green awning. After entering and checking his empty mailbox, he climbs the wide wooden steps to the second floor. Paintings from residents line the hallways. His building is occupied by artists, students, musicians, writers, and one cop, him.

At an open-house party a neighbor told Wyatt that he was the only resident with a normal job and Wyatt explained that detective work is not a normal job, that it consumes and changes people in much the way he imagined artistic pursuits can, sometimes in good ways, sometimes not. He was surprised to hear himself vocalize this and vowed not to get drunk with civilians again.

He turns the key in the lock of his door and quickly realizes it is not locked.

"Hello," he says, entering, wary.

His voice echoes through the long rectangular loft because of the concrete floors, the whitewashed brick walls, and the minimal furniture in the open space. He has lived here ten years and never bothered to furnish it with more than the essentials. A good friend of his, Mike Lawson, thinks that this is Zen, but Wyatt just calls it a low priority.

The hallway leads into one main room with four arched windows facing east over the bay and the industrialized tide flats and the dim orange lights of the port. Against the north wall is a desk with a laptop computer, steel bookshelves, a futon couch, and a stainless steel table where there is a paperback copy of Haruki Murakami's *Norwegian Wood*.

Nobody is home. His girlfriend, Suki, must have forgotten to lock the door again. The paperback and the futon are hers, along with the empty coffee cup. She has been living with him for more than a month and sometimes he wishes he still had his solitary space, but as he stands here alone now he unexpectedly misses her.

They have been together almost a year and he was on the verge of proposing at the nine-month mark. Instead he proposed that they move in together, buying time. Meanwhile, Howard has become the object of his attention.

For years Wyatt has lived by a simple code: work hard and pursue the truth and the center will hold and everything else will fall into place. Instead, things appear to be tearing apart in a storm of gray, and not quite fast enough to be fun.

He crosses over to his bookshelves and picks up a copy of *Moby-Dick*, brings it over to the futon. Sitting down, he opens the book, and inside the 1,011-page paperback is a carved-out compartment holding four artfully rolled joints. He places one in his mouth.

Preferring matches to lighters, he strikes one from a C.J.'s Bail Bonds pack and watches the flame for a moment before he touches it to the tip of the joint. After the excess paper burns off, he breathes in and fills his lungs.

The prickly sensation in his head from being on alert all day starts to subside into a low hum as he enjoys the sweet smell of a respite.

Though he is listening to one of Suki's CDs and reading *The Stranger* and thinking of Howard, he still hears the door open when she enters near midnight.

"Hi," he says from the futon, turning down the music with the remote.

"I'm glad you're still awake," she says, coming over and crawling onto the couch and kissing him.

"Me, too," he says after their lips separate.

"Listening to the Raveonettes?"

He nods. One of the advantages of having a girlfriend who is fourteen years younger is that she keeps him up to speed on new music, which happens to sound a lot like the old music, though the names have changed.

Half Japanese, half Scandinavian, with pale skin and large round eyes, Suki is always a welcome sight for him. She is wearing a red skirt and black tights and a white Strokes T-shirt.

Since his divorce he carried the hope that he would someday meet a girl like Suki, but then he found her and that was the end of the hope and it confused him that he missed having the hope. This made him wonder if the hoping wasn't better than the having.

He does not want to blow it this time.

"Did you notice anything about the door?" he asks.

"No."

"It was locked."

Suki starts laughing. "Oops, I guess you're telling me I *didn't* lock it?"

"Yes, we were robbed."

"That's unfortunate." She smiles slyly. "I'll just have to get a third job and pay you back."

They met at Cutter's Point, a coffee shop on the bottom floor of the building where Suki, a caffeine junkie, works as a barista. He dropped by to chat up a pretty barista named Erika, but one night Suki was working Erika's shift and Wyatt asked Suki out and forgot about Erika.

Suki, Wyatt was surprised to learn on their third date, also works at Foxes, one of Pierce County's several strip clubs. Because he formed his opinion of her before he knew she danced, he cannot picture her in this role. Suki is nothing like the strippers he has met who date other officers. She reads and is upbeat and does not do drugs.

An Army brat, Suki has lived all over the world, settling in Tacoma eleven years ago when she was thirteen. This was when she decided to be an actress. As an only child she was a prodigious reader: Anton Chekhov, Jane Austen, F. Scott Fitzgerald, Jack Kerouac, and later Mary Gaitskill. She wanted to be many things when she grew up—a journalist, a dancer, a veterinarian, a psychiatrist—and she realized she could be all these things and more as an actress, and also avoid a nine-to-five job.

She moved to Venice Beach after she graduated from high school and at first she loved it, the palm tress, the salt air, the smoggy orange chemical sunsets. *Just like in the movies,* she thought as many before her have. She took acting classes, met people, signed with an agent, appeared in three television commercials, and endured four and a half years of rejection, compromising proposals, and general soul-numbing nonsense until she decided to move back home to Tacoma.

Stripping seemed to her a natural progression. She is still acting, she tells herself, some nights playing a jaded tramp, other

nights playing a wide-eyed innocent, and almost every night playing a psychiatrist to the men who pay her more to sit with them
than to dance. She understands why they say she's an excellent
conversationalist: she listens.

Each month she puts at least two hundred dollars into her college savings fund, often more. Initially she wanted to attend Evergreen, but changed her mind when the small liberal arts college in
Olympia ignominiously invited a con-artist cop-killer to give a
taped commencement speech and Suki's Japanese-American
father, a staff sergeant in the U.S. Army, told her that Evergreen
was a school for "sheltered, spoiled fools." Suki knew this was an
overly broad condemnation, but still she turned her ambition to
the UW, Tacoma branch.

"Looks like you have the big book out," she says, eyeing
Melville's epic.

"Had a couple hits earlier."

"Long day?"

"And a long night, too. How was yours?"

"Some guy wanted me to talk pornglish to him," she says,
shrugging. "And I definitely couldn't get into it."

"You left early?"

"Yeah, bunch of kids without money tonight. Arriving in
packs. All saving their twenty dollars for a dance at the end of the
night. I didn't want to stick around for that grim finale. And, of
course, I missed you."

"Nice afterthought," he says, smiling.

They are both still adjusting to the pluses and minuses of living together and testing out new forms of communication that
accompany the change.

He tells her the story of the night and she is into it, laughing at his descriptions of Marvin's idiocy, but she turns serious when he gets to the part about Amber and her child.

"That's fucked up," she says. "I don't care if the tweekers want to ruin their lives, but why drag a child into that crap? Why have a child if that's how you're going to act? I don't get it."

Wyatt nods. "There's a lot of tweeker moms out there."

"That's fucked up." She slips off her ballet flats and stretches her legs out onto the coffee table. "I have a question."

"Of course."

"Who the hell is the Holy Ghost? We've got the Father, the Son, and the Holy Ghost, right? And the Father is God, and Jesus is the Son, but who the *hell* is the Holy Ghost?"

This is just the sort of question Suki, an inquisitive soul, occasionally comes up with and that he, as the almost omniscient detective, is supposed to answer.

"Internet?" he suggests, not sure about this one.

They pull office chairs on wheels around the flat computer screen and Wyatt surfs to the *Catholic Encyclopedia*. He and Suki were both raised Catholic under the influence of their mothers, though they are similarly casual about it and out of practice.

"'The Holy Ghost,'" Wyatt reads, 'is the spirit of God and at the same time the spirit of Christ.'"

"Okay," Suki says. "Is that it?"

Wyatt clicks to Bible.com for a second opinion. "The Holy Ghost is 'the comforter,'" he reads, "'the spirit God sends to earth.'"

"The comforter." Suki nods. "Okay, I like that." She pulls an Almond Joy from her purse. "I skipped dinner," she says, offering Wyatt a bite of the chocolate-covered almond and coconut candy.

He shakes his head. "How do you eat stuff like that and stay thin?"

"I don't believe a little piece like this can really be that many calories," she says, munching. "It's just a *little* piece."

This makes sense to Wyatt, though he suspects it should not.

"I have an idea," Suki says, "as long as we're here at the computer."

"Yes?"

"Vacation rentals in Kauai."

"Kauai? Why Kauai?"

"I saw it in that movie with you, *Honeymoon in Vegas*, and I've been picturing it a lot and I want to go there."

Wyatt thinks this a waste of time, as he has no idea when he would have enough time for vacation to justify a long and expensive trip, but Suki seems so excited at the prospect that he agrees and types search terms into Google.

Images of lush greenery, palm trees, deserted sandy beaches, and azure surf fill the screen and mesmerize them into a serene contemplation of paradise. A Corona commercial comes to mind for Wyatt.

"Heaven," Suki says.

"Yes," Wyatt agrees.

Many of the houses are inviting, but one stands out for Suki: Keahwaihi Hale, a glass-walled and green-tile-roofed home on Anini Beach with landscaped gardens. The interior is off-white and sea-foam green with fans hanging from the tan wood-beamed ceiling.

"Let's go!"

"Sure," he says.

"I'm serious. Ever since I met you, you've been talking about taking a vacation, but you never do it."

"I've taken some weekends off."

"And stayed here. You need to get away from this crime-is-everywhere mentality."

"Crime *is* everywhere, but especially here."

"Wyatt."

"Yes?"

"We've never taken a vacation together, even though you keep talking about it. What's up with that?"

Wyatt looks back at the screen. "You really want to go here?" he asks, clicking on more of the images.

"Yes!"

"That sounded . . . definite."

"I have two jobs. I want a vacation. I want to spend time with you."

"Okay, okay, I'll look into it tomorrow," he says, recognizing that he needs to be better about delivering on promises. "After I see when the house is available, and check my schedule at the office, and check my bank account. Cool?"

"Mahalo." She pauses. "What exactly does mahalo mean?"

Wyatt googles mahalo. "'Aloha and mahalo,'" he reads aloud. "'If you learn only two words in Hawaiian, learn these. Aloha is an invocation of the Divine and mahalo is a Divine blessing. Both are acknowledgments of the Divinity that dwells within and without.'"

"'Say them often, as they can be life-transforming and life-enhancing.'" Suki reads on. "'Be careful to use them only if you truly feel mahalo or aloha within. . . .'" Suki smiles at him. "I'll truly feel mahalo if we go there."

"Okay, it's a plan."

"Let's check Exit 133 or Creative Tacoma before we go to bed?"

Suki follows numerous blogs, and www.exit133.com and www.creativetacoma.com track what's happening in Tacoma and prove, she likes to tell Wyatt, that there are noncriminal activities.

"No, let's watch a movie," he says, turning off the computer, as her curiosity can keep them up for hours if unchecked. After watching Steven Spielberg's *Munich,* set in an era before she was born, they researched all night until it became too depressing. If Suki is intrigued by a movie, she likes to look up the writer and director on the Internet, seeking clues to the life experiences and history behind the screen story.

Both Wyatt and Suki are movie aficionados and their relationship, built on sensational sex in the beginning, has evolved into a cinema appreciation club. Stadium Video is a frequent date destination. Wyatt, to his surprise, does not mind.

"What do you want to watch?" he asks.

Suki expected a transition like this, as she has been through it before, sensing and studying the reaction of the man as she morphed from a fantasy who craves sex to a homebody who craves a vacation, her public self versus her truer self.

"*Blue Velvet*?" she suggests.

Set in Lumberton, a town that could be in rural Pierce County, the movie includes one of Wyatt's favorite lines, one that Suki immediately started quoting to him, "I can't figure out if you're a detective or a pervert."

Howard wonders if he should just walk right in and establish himself as the man of the house. Knocking, he fears, feels like the act of a stranger or a salesman.

As he steps up a gravel path through the overgrown grass of the front yard of the dilapidated rambler, he sees no lights. He recalls that Brandy's husband was usually armed, considers that he may have left guns behind.

Opening the broken screen door, he raps it quietly, then loudly. Water drips around him from the broken drainpipe on the porch.

"It's me," he yells. "Howard. Howard Schultz." However, he cannot remember if he was using that alias when he last saw Brandy, so he adds, "The King of Methlehem." If you say something often enough people will repeat it and it will thereby become so, Howard believes. The closest neighbor in this rural corner of the county is almost a football field away and so he yells it again, louder. *"The King of Methlehem!"*

After hearing nothing from inside the house, he walks around to the side where he thinks he remembers Brandy's bedroom was. He raps on the window, *tap, tap-tap-tap.*

"Who the goddamn fuck shit is it?" Brandy screeches. "I've got a gun."

"Me, it's just me, Howard, the king."

Moments later the curtain swings open and Brandy does indeed have a gun, a large handgun, which is pointing in his direction, and should, but does not, fully distract him from her breasts poking through a T-shirt. She lowers the gun as she slowly recognizes him.

He jabs his finger in the direction of the front door.

A few minutes later he is ranting in her living room about his escape from the cops, exaggerating and fictionalizing and making little sense.

"Could you keep your crazy-ass voice down? Kids are sleeping!"

He lowers his voice, but continues at the same babbling pace, sweating and burning off the last of the meth in his amped system, his feet tapping on the brown and orange shag rug, which is peppered with black cat hairs. When she gets a chance to speak she looks in his dilated eyes and asks the only thing she truly wants to know.

"Are you holding?"

"I did it all, had to. Maybe lost some, too."

"*All* of it?"

"You don't have any?"

"*Me?* I'm broke!"

"I'll cook again tomorrow," he says, assuring Brandy that he is of value to her. "Soon as the stores open."

"Okay." She brightens. "After the kids go to school."

"Does the car in the driveway run?"

"Not very well, but yes."

"What's wrong?"

"Carburetor or something, I don't know."

"Is the car yours?"

"It is now, I guess."

"How long is your boyfriend in jail for?"

"How did you know about that?"

"I keep up on the local news."

"He's got about two years left, including good time."

"He beat on you?"

"Yeah, and my boy Joe, too. Porsche called 911. He took a plea when he found out I was going to testify. If he hadn't kicked Joe around, I would have let it drop."

"He was a fuck," Howard says, finishing off a beer. "You deserve better."

"Yeah."

Her ex is a small-time dealer. One of the secrets of the drug trade is that when you add up the hours, dealing drugs pays below minimum wage—only the players at the top make real money. Still, there are plenty of applicants for entry-level positions. Not many other minimum-wage jobs are glorified in song and cinema.

"Did he leave you any money?" Howard asks.

"Are you fucking joking?"

"Guess not. How's your daughter doing? Porsche?"

"Who knows. She's a brat, screwing up in school. Kids today, they're a mess."

Howard nods in solemn agreement.

"And I haven't heard from her dad in years. He's in prison in California, I think."

Good. Howard nods.

"I should go back to bed," Brandy says, rising from the couch and setting down her beer with the other empties on the stained and cigarette-singed coffee table. "I have to go to work tomorrow."

"You have a *job?*"

"Waitressing," she says, coughing.

"You don't strip anymore?" he asks, disappointment in his voice.

"No, I quit Déjà Vu. That's a young girl's job." She stands. "I'm going back to bed. You can sleep on the couch."

"I'm going to stay up awhile, maybe work on the car."

Almost every tweeker house is accessorized by an old American automobile to tinker with. Howard attends to Brandy's, a 1972 black Camaro Z28 with rust spots. Reliable transportation is necessary for his future schemes and, more immediately, he feels the need to tweak with something, to stay outside his head, *to focus.*

Brandy's garage is filled with sundry junk, so the car is parked in the driveway. Ignoring the light rain, Howard begins disassembling various parts of the engine in the dim glow of the garage lights while vaguely imagining how Brandy's home makes a major meth operation possible.

By dawn he has the carburetor, air filter, fuel filter, and spark plugs lying in the driveway. He sits in the midst of the parts and fastidiously cleans them with gas siphoned from the tank.

Birds are chirping as Howard begins reassembling the carburetor and this proves fatally distracting. He cannot seem to remember what goes where and he blames this on the birds and when he throws a nut down in anger it bounces away into the tall grass, disappearing.

He is crawling around the yard, brushing open the grass with his grease-stained hands, when Porsche and her younger brother Joe walk out of the house and notice him.

Neither of the children seems particularly surprised to see a wild-eyed adult on all fours in the yard.

"Hi, Porsche," Howard says, standing, wiping his hands on his pants and leaving long black finger marks.

"Do I know you?"

Wearing jeans and a sweater, skinny and slouching, Porsche looks just as she did last year except taller, blonder, and with makeup. Ten is too young for Howard, but twelve, he quickly decides, is not. This is an aesthetic, rather than moral, choice.

Her little brother Joe is wearing black Dickies, a flannel shirt, and red shoelaces, which Howard recognizes as white supremacist garb.

"I'm Howard. I was staying with you for a while last time your dad was in prison."

"He's not my dad," she says.

"Your brother's dad." This exchange does not seem to spark a memory, so he adds, "I bought you clothes and . . . stuff."

"Oh, yeah," she says, nodding slowly. "Well, we gotta catch the bus."

"Your mom still asleep?"

"Probably."

Sleep, Howard suddenly realizes, is in his immediate future and he needs to prepare, needs to take the edge off before he comes down, before he *squishes*. He opens his wallet and pulls out a Klonopin, which he washes down with the backwash from a beer bottle. He prefers Klonopin to Xanax because Klonopin has a greater half-life and therefore keeps you under longer.

Twenty minutes later Howard is mildly nauseous, his twitches are less frequent, and his vision is blurring. He recognizes the Klonopin kicking in and gives up on reconstructing the engine parts he disassembled. All his schemes are temporarily forgotten.

Abandoning the mayhem of the driveway, he robotically marches into the house and finds Brandy's room. He tears off all his clothes, which are wet with rain and sweat, and crawls in beside her for a long dreamless crash.

"How many in-custodies?" Mike Lawson asks as he steps through the security door into the domain of the drug trial unit, arriving a few minutes before eight a.m. His workday officially runs from eight-thirty until four-thirty, but in practice is usually eight until six or seven or later, and he is never caught up.

The unit's six legal assistants are grouped together in cubicles near the entrance, surrounded by file cabinets and stacks of manila case files on the cabinets and floors and desks. His LAs process over two hundred cases a month, about ninety-eight percent of which will result in guilty pleas that involve over twenty pages of paperwork in triplicate.

"Twenty-seven," Kati says. "First eleven are on your desk."

"Thanks."

Twenty-seven defendants in Pierce County were arrested on drug charges yesterday, and today they must be charged or released. Reports will be skimmed, decisions will be quick. Mike walks down a cluttered hallway jammed with boxes of Xerox paper, file carts, recycling bins, and printers. He often thinks everyone will die if there is a fire.

The thirteen attorneys in the unit are housed in offices slightly smaller than jail cells, mostly two attorneys to an office, their desks side to side butting up against each other, files spilling over between them. At the end of the hallway is a poster of Martin Luther King with a quote: *Unarmed Truth Is the Most Powerful Thing in the Universe.*

But bet on armed truth, Wyatt once told Mike.

Mike's office, which is dominated by his oversized desk, has a view of downtown Tacoma and a black and white signed poster of Kurt Cobain with an acoustic guitar, *a cautionary tale.* Mike played bass guitar in a band before he went to law school.

When Mike walks in, Wyatt James is already sitting in one of the guest chairs, knees almost banging up against the desk. To Wyatt's left is a badly scarred metal file cabinet, standard government-issue.

"You still have a leak," Wyatt says, pointing to a brown-stained corner of the white acoustic tile.

"It's a slow one." Mike hangs up his raincoat and suit jacket behind the door. "You look like you haven't slept for a while."

"Business is brisk. What happened with the lab they found last week at that trailer in South Prairie?"

"Couldn't charge it."

"Problematic search," Wyatt guesses.

"No warrant, no exigent circumstances."

"How bad?"

"The Gestapo would blush."

"Marcello?"

"Yeah."

"Marcello's a good cop, just a little overeager. I'll talk to him. He felt bad about that lawsuit."

"Which one?"

"Both, but especially the one where he got the lab address wrong, and the elderly neighbor freaked out when his door was kicked down."

"You mean the heart attack?"

"Come on, it wasn't an actual heart attack. The guy just fainted is all. He was fine."

"After receiving his out-of-court settlement."

"Living near tweekers is hazardous."

Mike logs in to his computer. The windows are streaked with rain and you cannot see anything outside but fuzzy outlines of buildings that look like they are melting.

Death has been on Mike's mind of late, his own in particular, but also in general, and it does not take much to trigger the morbidity. Clouds, for example, bring it on, which is problematic when you live in the Pacific Northwest, the cloudiest corner of the country.

"Couldn't sleep last night," Mike says, "so I watched *Cool Hand Luke* again."

"Excellent."

"Best line besides 'What we've got here is a failure to communicate'?"

"'You're going to get your head right, Luke.'"

This is one of their rituals. Sometimes they will riff on and on, until they agree on the best line, but Mike cannot think of another quotable line this morning. His mind is already calculating the miscellaneous tasks ahead.

"So what's up?" he asks as he continues to wait for the outdated government computer to power up.

"I want to try to turn a couple defendants into informants, including a woman from a recent trailer lab. Tweekers who probably don't meet your criteria."

"Probably don't?"

"Okay. Definitely don't."

Mike nods, indicating a willingness to at least listen to Wyatt's pitch, despite the din outside his open door as support staff looking for files and attorneys prepping for court pass back and forth chattering. Someone is always looking for something lost.

Wyatt has known Mike for almost twelve years, going back to when Mike was an aggressive twenty-eight-year-old just out of law school. Many rookie prosecutors annoy Wyatt with their self-importance and power trips, but he liked Mike, found him to be a kindred spirit. Mike was older than most freshmen and he looked and acted like Wyatt believes a prosecutor should: blue suit, white shirt, passionate about the cause but not psychotically so.

However, Wyatt laments Mike's promotion to team chief. Becoming a supervisor is the worst thing that can happen to a detective or a trial attorney, in Wyatt's opinion. They suddenly have to consider how the herd will react to their every move.

Kati enters and drops a few more files in the bin. "Bail returns," she explains apologetically. "We're up to thirty-one. Looks like about six are labs." On her way out she adds, "Oh, and the Xerox machine is broken again."

"This is about Howard," Wyatt explains after she leaves.

"Your white whale."

"In the last week we've taken down a couple people who can get us close to him."

"You figured out his real name yet?"

"We're sticking with Beelzebub for now."

One of the trial attorneys pokes his head into the office. "Twenty-seven in-custodies?"

"I thought you were in trial."

"Defendant didn't show."

"Grab one, thanks."

He nods to Wyatt, takes a couple files out of the tall stack in the bin on Mike's desk, and disappears.

"Thanks," Mike says, grabbing one himself.

"You want me to come back later," Wyatt asks, "when it's less crazy?"

"I'm not going to be here at midnight."

"Okay, I'll try to keep this quick. Both of these characters could be good informants, but the guy has an Assault One pending, as well as some domestic violence convictions, and the woman is charged with Endangerment of a Minor with a Controlled Substance."

Wyatt holds up his hand as Mike is about to speak. "I know you wouldn't want to normally work either of these two, but they're high-value, potentially at least. The guy led us to one of Howard's guerrilla trailer labs, we only missed him by a few minutes. And the girl, we found her there, with her kid."

Mike's head fills with headlines from the *News Tribune: Prosecutor Gives Violent Criminal a Free Pass, Prosecutor Says No Jail for Meth Mom,* and then suddenly he's standing in front of a news camera stammering out a mea culpa.

"If you could," the reporter asks, "would you take back this horrific fuckup?"

"Can't do it, Wyatt. We have guidelines for informants."

"Rules are made to be bent, Counselor."

"That's fine talk for an officer of the law."

"If you're investigating the devil, you don't go to heaven for witnesses."

"Nice line, but I'm not going to give meth mom a free pass right back to where she was. Maybe we can discuss it again after she's been clean for a few weeks."

Wyatt takes a pause, considers angles. "Let me tell you about the guy, Marvin."

Cort, the assistant supervisor, enters, still wearing his blue raincoat, his short hair wet. "Did you watch TV last night?" he asks, apparently outraged. "There's a new show on called *UnJustice* or something, and it's based on *The Innocence Project,* that whore Barry Scheck's self-promotion project."

"Barry Scheck?" Wyatt says. "The O.J. guy?"

"The very one," Cort says. "This show nearly made me vomit. It takes the ten- to twenty-year appeal process, reduces it to nine days so there's a 'ticking clock' "—he makes quotes in the air with his fingers—"and they actually rip pages off a calendar as each day passes. There are too many clichés to list, the acting is worse than the Shopping Channel, and the writers know nothing about the criminal justice system. They think sua sponte is an Italian ice cream."

Wyatt and Mike laugh as Cort continues his rant.

"Kyle McLachlan is the star, and he totally debases himself, playing a corporate lawyer with political ambitions who thinks he can become the attorney general or something by . . . freeing 'innocent convicted people'—he makes quotes in the air again— and so the show takes the most contrived, ridiculous, laughable conspiracy theories you've ever heard desperate defense attorneys make up, and then alters reality so the ridiculous conspiracy theory turns out to be . . . *true!*" He shakes his head. "It's going to totally poison our jury panels."

"Don't worry," Mike says. "I'm going to start my own TV show. It will focus on the victims of the hundreds of child molesters, rapists, meth cooks, and murderers who walk free on technicalities. We'll call it *The Guilt Project.*"

"How about if a detective," Wyatt suggests, getting into it, "say . . . me, hunts them down and shoots them?"

"All true stories end in death."

"I like it," Cort says, picking up half a dozen files from the bin before leaving for his own office directly across the hall.

"Life in a MASH unit," Mike says. "Tell me about Marvin."

"Assault case pending. Public service shooting. Shot another tweeker with the guy's own gun when they were playing with it. It was a total accident."

"Accident?"

"Yeah, I know it sounds like bullshit, but I looked into it and Marvin's too wimpy to shoot anyone intentionally."

"And the DV?"

"Misdemeanors."

"I hate putting wife-beaters on contract. You never know when they'll go ballistic and kill some woman."

"This guy is a twerp."

"They usually are."

"If you want a tweeker informant, you're going to have to work with wife-beaters, because meth and DV go together like rum and Coke at a high school prom."

Mike leans back in his chair, breathes in deeply.

A drop of water falls from the ceiling onto the rug near Wyatt's feet. He can feel the no coming, but he does not want Mike to say it, so he changes the subject.

"The leak doesn't bother you?"

"I'm used to it."

"I think it would get to me."

"Listen, I appreciate where you're coming from on this," Mike finally says, and Wyatt immediately pegs this as supervisor-speak, and again cuts him off before he can say no.

"I like the straight-arrow thing you've got going for you now, Mike, I really do," Wyatt says. "But you're not prosecuting sex crimes anymore. You're working in the drug world, and it's all about informants, and they're all unpredictable, they're all risky. They're all fucking *criminals.*"

Mike nods, missing the days when he was simply a trial lawyer without supervisory responsibility.

"Don't answer now," Wyatt says. "Just think about it. Okay?"

"But we don't know enough about this character. He sounds

like just another garden-variety meth maggot. Nobody worth risking our reputations on."

"*What* reputations? I'm known as a troublemaker."

"Okay, he's not important enough to risk *my* reputation."

"Which I understand is the important thing here."

"Exactly."

"Need help with charging?"

Another deputy prosecutor quickly grabs a couple files from the in-box and goes back to her office across the hall before Mike can even answer.

"What happened to your trial?" he calls out to her.

"Defense attorney didn't show," she yells back.

Mike shrugs to Wyatt: *If it's not one thing, it's another.*

"You believe in signs," Wyatt says.

"Yes, sometimes."

"Communication from the nonmaterial world?"

"Yes?"

"Well, I got a sign on this case, Mike. I swear to fucking God."

"A sign?"

"A Starbucks cup."

Mike stares, trying to gauge his seriousness.

"I mean it," Wyatt says, knowing Mike's look.

"The thing about signs is this," Mike says. "You have to be careful not to misinterpret them."

"You're always worried that using informants is going to blow up, I know."

"I'll just explain to the media that you had a sign. A Starbucks cup. They'll understand."

"I'll take the hit if something goes sideways. You know I'm one of the king's men and I don't want to do anything to hurt your election chances."

"My boss is elected," Mike says. "Not me."

"Just thinking ahead, chief. Like you do."

Politically, the prosecutor's office is a napping giant, but Wyatt recognizes that there are unspoken plans for a wake-up. Politics, as far as Wyatt can tell, is just a matter of understanding and liking people. However, unlike Mike, Wyatt believes these qualities are mutually exclusive.

Another deputy prosecutor steps into the office, breathing heavy, one hand holding multiple files, one hand on his chest.

"You look like you've been shot," Wyatt says.

"Two of the elevators are out," he explains between breaths. "I took the stairs from five, where I saw that reporter from the *News Tribune*. She's looking for you, Mike. She wants a quote on the Bush administration's latest."

"Her name's Karen. What latest?"

"They're taking money from meth prosecution and putting it into marijuana." He removes the hand from his chest and grabs a file for charging on his way out. "Just wanted to give you a heads-up."

"Ignoring cancer," Mike says, "fighting the head cold."

"Follow the money," Wyatt says. "We raid a marijuana grower, we find SUVs and loads of cash. We raid a meth lab, we find blue tarps and porn."

Another deputy prosecutor steps in, frazzled. "When you have a second, Mike, I have to talk to you about this issue that came up in trial. I want to kill the judge."

"Bad idea," Mike says.

"I have definitely *not* reached a state of Zen on this case."

"Give me half a minute here."

"Thanks," he says, picking up a file for charging.

"No," Mike says, "you're still in trial, right?"

"Right," he says, setting the file back. He walks out muttering, exhibiting symptoms of shell-shock, a common sight in a trial unit.

"Okay, I'll let you get back to work," Wyatt says, standing and looking over Mike's head at the poster. "But you know what Cobain said about this sort of situation?"

"'A mosquito, my libido'?"

"'The worst crime is faking it.' We need to go after Howard and those guys, really try to put the stake through their hearts. Either that or quit pretending like we're doing something."

A gust of wind whistles across the window, smearing the rain in streaks. Another drop falls from the ceiling.

"We've got two choices here," Mike says. "Find a semi-clean informant, or find evidence that this Howard Schultz character is worth the risk. What makes him different from the hundreds of other cooks?"

"Well, he's ambitious. He's like you in that way."

Home around eight p.m., Mike has a handful of peanuts and scotch straight up for dinner while he reads the *News Tribune*. He lives a long walk from the courthouse, near Stadium High School, the coolest school building he has ever seen, a gothic castle that was featured in the movie *10 Things I Hate About You*. Mike, who graduated from Bellarmine Prep, believes high school would have been a finer aesthetic experience in such a structure.

Environment matters.

After polishing off the peanuts, still wearing his blue suit, raincoat, and wingtips, he steps out into the backyard of his 1920 Craftsman home. Just off his deck is a long green lawn he uses for drunken croquet in the summer.

At the end of the lawn is a rock garden Mike installed himself, an oval bed of swirling furrows of raked round pebbles, partially surrounded by Japanese maple trees with wet orange and yellow leaves covered with raindrops that glisten in the porch light. There are two boulders on the edges on the rock garden for sitting, and a pedestal birdbath in the middle. Carrying a scotch, smoking an unfiltered Camel, Mike walks across the wet grass and stops at the edge and focuses on the birdbath.

Tiny sporadic raindrops plop into the dark water.

Though he does not particularly like birds, Mike bought the birdbath because of an experience he had at a girlfriend's house in college. One morning, hungover, hoping to clear his head, he was sipping coffee in the backyard and blankly gazing at a birdbath when an epiphany swept over him.

There was sunshine on the horizon but a light rain falling,

and he was watching the concentric circles from the falling drops when suddenly he had a flowing sensation that rose from his feet and possessed his body and then his mind. Suddenly the chaos that had been perplexing him melted and was replaced by a calm understanding that everything was ordered, everything was connected, everything was cool. For the seconds it lasted it was bliss.

He did not know what to make of this.

After college, when he was in the band and had extra time on his hands, Mike studied Shotokan karate and his sensei encouraged him to begin meditating. He considered several mantras, including Rama, which unfortunately put him in mind of Top Ramen noodles. He decided to skip the mantra and concentrate on breathing, and this was relaxing and centered him but never brought him to the bliss he had experienced staring into the ex-girlfriend's birdbath.

Lack of commitment is what doomed his band, in Mike's estimation, and since the failure of the band Mike decided he would not do anything without total commitment. Thus he pursued his interest in the spiritual world as a devoted student, something he had never been in college.

In his search to find a code to live by he bought numerous books, including Zen books, *The Way of Zen* by Alan Watts, *Zen for Americans* by Soyen Shaku, translated by D. T. Suzuki, *Zen and the Art of Archery* by Eugen Herrigel, *Zen and the Art of Motorcycle Maintenance* by Robert Pirsig, *Zen and the Art of Poker* by Larry W. Phillips, and his favorite title, *"Don't Just Do Something, Sit There* by Sylvia Boorstein.

After the Zen binge, he turned to *The Varieties of Religious Experience* by William James, a Kierkegaard anthology and some Schopenhauer, all of Hemingway, which he enjoyed, and Dostoyevsky, which he did not realize he enjoyed until years later.

These books led him to law school and then the Prosecuting Attorney's office because there are not many occupations where the job description is a search for the truth and the paycheck is regular. As novelist Tom Robbins wrote, there is "a certain Buddhistic calm" that comes with having a job and money in the bank.

As far as Mike could determine, the goal of Zen is enlightenment, or satori, and ultimately Nirvana, which, according to Merriam-Webster online, is "the cessation of desire." This perplexed Mike for months. He played the following cross-examination out in his head repeatedly.

Me: The goal of Zen is Nirvana?

Buddha: Yes.

Me: Nirvana includes the cessation of desire?

Buddha: Yes.

Me: Reaching Zen means no longer wanting anything.

Buddha: Yes.

Me: So if you have reached Zen, you don't even want to be Zen?

Buddha stares back, smiling beatifically, cryptic and fat and infuriating.

Mike gave up meditating for a while, *never mind Nirvana,* though he still recommended Zen to his colleagues as a way to temper the maddening absurdities of the criminal justice system.

Hard work became his religion, and it occupied more hours than any church. He gave up activities that took time away from work, most of which, such as television and golf, he did not miss, and some, such as reading and dating, he did. He attributed his courtroom successes to relentless work, though it came to him naturally.

When the stress of a prosecutor's endless caseload began causing him to lose sleep and grind his teeth and was threatening to take over his life, he returned to meditation and added another title to his shelf, *Meditation for Dummies* by Stephan Bodian.

Bodian posits the idea that there are four popular ways to deal with the noise of the modern world: addiction, consumerism, fundamentalism, and entertainment, all of which are flawed because they are one-dimensional, increase alienation, and do not enrich one's soul.

Based on his experience observing addicts in the criminal justice system, fundamentalists in politics, and consumerists in the legal and civilian communities, all of whom seem remarkably similar, Mike mostly agrees.

Entertainment he can not join Bodian in condemning because Mike loves movies and music and literature and he is convinced these things are good and help him face death.

Accepting death is on his to-do list.

His cupped cigarette becomes soggy in the drizzle, and he drops it, grinds it out with his wingtip. *Advantage of unfiltered smokes: biodegradable and good for the lawn.*

He stares at the birdbath and sips his scotch until the glass is empty and his head is dripping wet, bliss eluding him once again.

Stiff and sore, Howard struggles out of bed after being down for nearly thirty hours, an entire day lost. Though the jittery anxiety of the day before yesterday is gone, it is replaced by a numb depression Howard likes even less. His mind feels like mud.

Taking heavy and awkward steps, he staggers into the kitchen and he is relieved to see Brandy at the kitchen table eating cereal. Rotting apples and bananas sit in a Tupperware bowl in the center of the table.

"Eating . . ." he says, voice hoarse, the rest of the sentence fading away.

"Good morning."

"Do you . . . like . . . have . . . baby food?"

"Baby food?" She frowns. "No."

"Gate . . . Gatorade?"

"No."

"Mountain Dew?"

"No."

"We *need* Mountain Dew."

He sits down across from her, arms on the table, shoulders slumped. Outside it is another gray fall day. Through dirty sliding glass doors he can see an unkempt backyard of dirt and crabgrass that stretches out to a dilapidated barn with faded and cracked red paint.

"What time is it?" he asks.

"A little after one."

"I need some food."

"What do you want?"

"What?"

"What? Nothing."

He's going to call the cops, Howard thinks as he walks out the door, and he looks over his shoulder from the parking lot, and sure enough the clerk is on the phone.

Suspicious prick.

Taking the keys from his teenage driver, making sure nobody sees him, Howard stashes his purchases in the trunk because cops cannot open it without a warrant. When he was just starting in the business he had a meth lab case dismissed because the officer opened his unlocked trunk.

Though in the good old days it would be extremely unlikely that the sheriff's department would have the time or inclination to respond to a clerk's suspicions, it seems to Howard that lately *everyone* is on the lookout for meth labs, *it's a clampdown.*

Next stop, Home Depot, and Howard picks up lithium batteries, drain cleaner, and rock salt, again tossing the goods into the trunk. Rarely does he pick up three items in one store, but he's jonesing and so is Brandy and so is his driver and Howard wants to deliver soon, wants to be *the man.*

At Rite-Aid, Howard sends the teenage driver inside for two boxes of Sudafed, the legal limit. Howard and Brandy wait in the car because of the logbook customers must sign to purchase pseudoephedrine. On the Internet Howard followed the legislative battle that accompanied the law that created these restrictions and was surprised to see the retailers, who had billions of dollars at stake, lose the battle.

Pfizer, the company best known for Viagra, also manufactures Sudafed. Sales of Sudafed and other pseudoephedrine products began climbing at an astronomical rate as Nazi labs proliferated across the country in the eighties and nineties. Pfizer

"A banana that's not . . . brown?"

"Don't have any. I'd go get you something, but you took the fucking car apart yesterday."

"I can fix it . . . better."

"I missed work because of you."

"Because of me. Who?"

"Because my fucking car isn't running."

"I told you, I'll fix the . . . car."

"You going to cook today? I need to zoom."

Brandy has been off meth for months, but with Howard around it is all she can think about, that rush. His presence makes meth seem imminent, like the dark clouds that portend rain.

Howard wipes his nose, looks around the kitchen. On the wall near the stove is a land line. He shoves back his chair, groaning, and crosses over and picks up the phone to call a client.

"Requisition mission," he says, giving the client instructions on where to pick him up—an intersection about a mile from the house because he does not want a loose-lipped tweeker to know where he is staying.

Brandy and Howard wait by the side of the road, tapping their feet and rubbing their hands. The client, a long-haired pimply-faced teenager whose name Howard cannot remember, drives up in an early seventies black Firebird with a hood that is half gray primer paint and half fire-breathing bird. Tweeker cars are always a work in progress.

First they stop at Schuck's, park in back. Howard purchases Heet and automobile starter fluid, and the clerk looks uneasy as he rings up the purchases, possibly because Howard is shaking and sweating on a cold morning.

"Car issues," Howard says, sensing suspicion, but it comes out sounding like "Carissa."

and other pharmaceutical companies are more profitable than the drug cartels and they do not have to pay off or kill police to stay in business.

Howard trusts the pharmaceuticals will find a way to keep the supply lines open.

What's good for business is good for America.

About a mile down the road they stop at a Safeway and once again Howard instructs the teenager to purchase two boxes of Sudafed.

"You have to show ID," he says. "They made me show my license at the Rite-Aid."

"Don't you think I fucking know that?" Howard reaches into a pocket of his jeans and hands the kid a Washington driver's license for Peter Farrelly, the director of *Dumb and Dumber,* one of Howard's favorite movies. Farrelly has salt-and-pepper hair and a goatee.

"That doesn't look like me," the driver says.

"Do you think the minimum-wage slave working here cares?"

"I dunno."

"Well, they don't. I've used that ID plenty."

"Maybe we should go to the chink store instead?"

"Cops shut it down."

"You'll do fine," Brandy says. "You have an innocent face."

An innocent zit-face, Howard almost adds.

Bolstered by Brandy's confidence, the driver completes his assignment in Safeway, skipping out of the store with the boxes held high like a trophy.

A few minutes later they are on their way to one more store, mission almost accomplished, but they are lit up from behind: flashing lights and a siren burst.

"Fuck."

"Fuck!"

"Fucking *shit*," Howard says. "Don't panic. Did you forget to signal your turn?"

"I don't know, maybe. Fuck."

"Turn on your windshield wipers."

"It's not raining."

"Yes, it is."

"No, it's not!"

"Maintain! Everyone just *maintain*."

All three light up Kools, and the car quickly fills with smoke like a scene from a Cheech and Chong movie.

"What should I do?" the driver asks, speed unchanged.

"What should you do? What do you think? Pull over, you idiot."

"Right, sure, that's a good idea, I guess."

"Fucking maintain."

"Maintain?"

"Act like you haven't done anything wrong," Howard says. "And shove the bags under your seat."

"Right," the driver says, hands shaking as one foot presses the brake and the other foot clumsily kicks the bags from Rite-Aid and Safeway under his bucket seat.

Deputy Newton, a twenty-one-year-old rookie, approaches the driver's-side window. "Are you aware that your left taillight is broken?" the deputy asks. He has freckles and looks as though he just started shaving.

"No, Officer," the driver says between nervous puffs.

"Please put out the cigarette."

After the driver does so, the deputy asks him for his driver's license, registration, and proof of insurance. Providing one out of three, his license, the driver apologizes profusely.

"I think my license might be suspended."

"You don't know?"

"I'm pretty sure it is."

"Been shopping?" the deputy asks as he scans the interior the cluttered car, *the usual meth mess.*

"No."

"No?" The deputy points to the bags on the floorboard poking out from under the driver's seat, the Sudafed packages visible through the plastic. "You sure?"

"Oh, yeah."

"Rite-Aid?"

"Yes."

"Anyplace else?"

"No."

"You were coming from the Safeway parking lot."

"Oh, yeah, well, that's right. Rite-Aid and then Safeway because . . . they didn't have everything I needed."

"What didn't they have?"

The driver stares back at the deputy while Howard is thinking *moron* so loud he's surprised he cannot be heard.

"Let me guess," the deputy finally says when no answer is forthcoming. "Cold medicine?"

"I'm not feeling well." The driver coughs, wipes the sweat off his forehead.

"How many boxes?" the deputy asks.

"Just two."

"At each store?"

"Right. I mean, no. Two total. I was looking for Sudafed and they only had one box at Rite-Aid and so we went to Safeway for more."

"More?"

"Just two more."

"That would make three."

"I mean one more, two total."

As the deputy looks over at him, Howard sits silent, controlling his twitching as much as he can, thinking over and over, *Why must I live my life surrounded by morons?*

"You want to show me there's only one box in the bag?" the deputy says, turning his attention back to the driver.

"I think it's only one."

"So it might be two in each bag?"

"I don't know. I don't remember."

"Sounds like there might be two in each bag."

"Okay, yeah, maybe."

"Who bought them?"

Howard, for the first time, moves his head and speaks up. "We're just hitchhikers," he says. "This kid offered us a ride in the parking lot, out to... Orting. We don't really know him."

"That's true," the driver says on cue.

That's bullshit, the deputy thinks. "So who bought the boxes?" he asks the driver.

"I did."

"Four boxes for yourself?"

"I guess so, yeah."

"Today?"

"Yeah."

"Do you know it's against the law to buy more than two packages of pseudoephedrine in a twenty-four-hour period?"

"Yeah, I mean, no."

After arresting the driver for the misdemeanor and placing him in the patrol car, he clears the passengers out to the side of the road and commences a search of the car. He finds withered french fries, coffee cups, cigarette butts, candy bar wrappers, and endless junk, but no evidence beyond the four full packages of Sudafed and several empty pseudo packages, presumably from previous smurfing, as the purchasing of large numbers of pseudo packages is known in the trade.

As strings of rain begin falling, he walks back to the patrol car and asks the driver if anything is in the trunk.

"A spare tire, I think."

"Anything illegal?"

"Not that I know of."

"So there might be?"

Not wanting to fall down that slippery slope again, the driver quickly says, "No, sir."

"Whose car is it?"

"A friend's."

"What's your friend's name?"

After a long pause the driver says, "Hugh."

"Hugh."

"Yeah, Hugh." His head nods rapidly. "That's his name."

"Hugh what?"

"Hugh ... don't know."

"Of course."

For a moment there's a silent standoff. The deputy lacks probable cause for a warrant to get into the trunk, and the driver has gone into denial mode.

"Can we go now?" Howard asks, still standing on the side of the road with Brandy, pulling out his cell phone to call a taxi, knowing the deputy cannot even ask for ID from a passenger.

I know my rights, he gloats silently.

Holed up at a Lakewood motel that Howard paid for with a stolen credit card, he and Brandy sit on the bed hunched over a mirror he tore off the bathroom wall, clothes wet, heat on high, sweating. Their sinuses are sufficiently damaged that they cannot smell each other.

Howard methodically cuts the off-white lines with a Swiss Army knife as Brandy stares, her eyes jerking back and forth as she watches.

"Would you fucking hurry up?"

"Would you fucking shut up?"

"I'm sorry, I just don't wanna squish."

"Don't act like a bag 'ho."

Delaying consciously now, he chops the powder up for another thirty seconds, meticulously shaping two lines to the side of the pile. Moving slowly, he snorts up one of the lines with a dollar bill.

"*Please*," Brandy says. "I'm *really* sorry."

He hands her the bill and she quickly hoovers up the other line. "Holy Mother of fucking Christ," she says, reeling her head back. "That's *harsh*."

"It's been stepped on, fucking Mexican crank."

Howard hates buying from competitors, but he needed a boost after the kid was busted, and so he tracked down an identity thief who sometimes deals from the motel. Their room is dirty beige and orange and on the wall above the bed is an amateurish painting of a cowboy sitting on a horse in a field looking out at a sun setting over a distant mountain.

As Howard loses his high, he starts to get into his head and this is the last place in the world he wants to be, *can't go there, can't go there.*

"Here's the plan," he says, looking up, wiping his nose. "Like what's-his-name said, the 'times are a-changing.' They're keeping logbooks on pseudo purchases, following the runners, busting people, turning them into snitches. Smurfing has become too dangerous."

Brandy has no idea what Howard is babbling about, but she can sense it is important to him and so she nods encouragingly.

"Yeah?"

"Absolutely."

"Are you going to cut more lines?"

"I have to do something to deal with the changes," he says, bending over, slicing up a new set of lines. "Here's what I do. I got the know-how, I got the clients, I got the distribution network. I just need to start a major cook operation. No more of these little guerrilla labs, but a big-time lab."

"Where?" Brandy asks, thinking a response is required.

"Your place."

"My place?"

"The barn." He lifts the knife off the mirror and points at the line nearest Brandy. "All I need is a pseudo supplier, someone with serious access, so I can do some serious cooking. I mean, I'm almost thirty-three, it's time for me to do something with my life."

Brandy leans forward with the dollar bill and snorts up the line and it is less painful this time but she still makes a face and shakes her head.

"So what do you think?" he asks.

"Fucking harsh."

"About the plan."

"The plan?"

"Big labs are the next wave. And I'm going to be riding it." He juts his arms out as though he's up on a surfboard. "What do you fuckin' think?"

Brandy wipes her nose, breathes in raggedly, her white-crusted nostrils flaring.

"You think a lot," she finally says.

He nods. "Yep."

"More people should," she adds. "Thinking's good. I've always liked that about you."

"That's why I'm the King of Methlehem. And now you're going to be the queen."

The future queen greedily leans down for the other line and it all sounds good in the moment.

FOOD FOR THOUGHT

Over two hundred people line up under the freeway overpass near the Tacoma Dome every Friday night, some homeless, some low-income, some in wheelchairs or on crutches, many with their children.

Volunteers in orange safety vests hold them in a semi-orderly line on the north side of Twenty-fourth Street while a diverse group of do-gooders set up tables in a parking lot on the other side of the street and load the tables with blankets, clothes, sandwiches in plastic baggies, boxes of cereal, apples, and Bibles.

Diesel generators provide the electricity for the bright construction-site lights that flood the area with a warm glow, and for the amplifiers of the surprisingly tight band that plays everything from folk tunes to Christian rock to Bruce Springsteen.

Pastor Ed and Pastor Jack are the chief organizers of this event, though they deny the organization is by design. People show up to give out food and clothes, and other people show up to receive food and clothes. That's all there is to it, they say, along with the most important thing: *God's will.*

On his way to reconnoiter the Friday Night Feed, Wyatt stops at the Tacoma Book Center two blocks away, a used book store in a one-story brick building. The windows are boarded up. Out front on a cart, when it is not raining, there are books offered up for twenty-five cents, including some good ones.

Inside, the air is musty and stale and the lighting dim, but Wyatt can spend hours browsing. He keeps a close eye on his watch so this does not happen. After a few minutes he finds a Murakami novel he thinks Suki has not yet read, *A Wild Sheep Chase,* and buys it for four dollars.

Wyatt has blown countless relationships in his life and wants this one to be different. He does not quite know yet what makes a relationship work, but he knows that little gestures help, and indifference is death.

Placing the paperback in his blazer pocket, protecting it from the light drizzle, he walks down Dome Street across the railroad tracks. At Twenty-fourth he takes a left toward the Feed.

Tweekers do not usually attend the Feed, as food is not a priority, but when Marvin is out of money he withdraws from meth and develops an appetite. As Wyatt circles the parking lot he spots Marvin on the fringe with a fidgety group, not quite in line, wearing a ragged overcoat. The men around him scatter like a covey of quail as Wyatt approaches.

Marvin is about to bolt, too, but Wyatt freezes him in place with eye contact. "Hi, Marvin."

"What's up?"

"I have to arrest you on a warrant."

"Oh, man. No, you said . . . no, *man.*"

Wyatt snaps the cuffs on as bystanders watch, accustomed to the sight. A preteen girl in a jean jacket scrutinizes the process with particular attention. Wyatt smiles at her reassuringly, but all he gets back from her is a cold stare. He suspects her parents have not told her good things about the police.

"Man," Marvin says, "you told me—"

"Shut up."

When they have walked far enough away from the crowd Wyatt explains that he just wants to talk, but had to arrest Marvin so his friends would not suspect he is a snitch.

"Oh. Thanks, man."

"You're welcome."

"So the warrant is squashed?"

"No, the warrant's still outstanding."

They continue to walk toward the Taurus so that Wyatt can drive him away and minimize suspicion. Marvin would otherwise just return to the Feed and gab.

"I thought you were going to squash the warrant on that assault case," he says.

"The prosecutor wasn't willing to put you on contract. Not yet."

"Why not?"

"Because you have a shitty criminal history."

"Doesn't everybody?"

"Yeah, well, not quite as bad as yours. You've got that Assault One."

"It was an accident!"

"Yeah, you've told me, but we're going to have to promise the prosecutor something big you can deliver."

Wyatt is so used to lying to defendants about this sort of thing—playing the good cop to the prosecutor's bad cop—he worries that he might sound different telling the truth.

"Like what?" Marvin asks.

"I want to know what Howard has his hands in, besides cooking."

"Everything."

"What do you mean, 'everything'?"

"Like cooking and identity theft and stolen property and stuff?"

"Was that a statement or a question?"

Marvin pauses. "What do you mean?"

"Tell me about his involvement in identity theft."

"Well, he knows dozens of tweekers and he sometimes trades meth to them for stolen identities, and sometimes he hires people."

"Hires people to do what?"

"Steal shit, steal identities. They usually go bad quick, the identities, people report it, so there's like a constant demand for new ones."

"Can I prove it?"

"Prove what?"

"That he's an identity theft ringleader."

"Everybody knows he's into identity theft."

"What do you think would happen if a prosecutor called me to give evidence in a trial and all I said was, 'Everybody knows he's into identity theft?' "

Marvin thinks hard about this. "The guy would go to jail?" he finally answers.

"True, but that's not my point." Wyatt wonders if Marvin's brain will ever return to full functionality. "My point is that the prosecutor wants proof, something more than hearsay."

"And you'll squash the warrant if I give you something? Proof?"

"Yes, and the word is *quash*. You quash a warrant."

A DIRTY, POORLY LIT PLACE

Soft daylight streams into the barn through cracks, knotholes, and missing side planks, illuminating ragged spiderwebs throughout. The space is slightly larger than a two-car garage, and the tall double doors open wide. Against the far side is a rusting refrigerator, a wheelbarrow, an ancient lawn mower, and a long and worn wooden workbench.

Kicking the dirt with the heel of his cowboy boot he announces, "This is it, this is where Pierce County history is going to be made."

Howard is confident that this is one of the qualities that lift him above his loser peers: foresight.

Brandy, standing beside him, looks around. They have been zooming for a couple days and she is shaking and feels the squish coming on.

"There's no electricity," she points out. "Or anything, really."

"That's why it's perfect."

He is so pumped up, Brandy's suspicious.

"If you had any more now you would share it, right?"

"Baby, of course. We did it all. And I'm not high anymore," he lies. "I'm just . . . *into* this."

"You'll have to get rid of the fucking spiderwebs or I'm never coming out here again."

"Let's get the kids."

"For what?"

"To help us push the car."

Porsche steers the Camaro up the muddy dirt driveway to the barn while Howard, Brandy, and Joe shove on the rear, slipping occasionally as they try to keep their momentum going through the shallow puddles along the way. Joe, wearing surplus military boots, has the best traction.

"Don't stop," Howard warns, "don't stop or we'll be stuck."

"Why are we doing this?" Joe asks.

"This is going to be my work area," Howard explains. "My private work area. For fixing the car and other stuff."

"Why didn't you fix the car where it was," Joe asks, "and then you could *drive* it here?"

"Nobody likes a smart-ass, Joe," Brandy says.

"Fuck you," he mutters.

"Fuck *you*," Howard says, slapping the top of his head.

"Hey," Joe says, "you can't do that."

"Yes, I can." Howard whaps Joe's head again. "We're like a family now!" Family is a remote concept to Howard. His only memory of his father is some domestic violence before he left, and shortly thereafter his sister was taken by Child Protective Services—*the goddamn government*—for reasons that were never explained to him, and his mother, he once heard as a child, was the "the whore of Tate Estates." Tate Estates was the trailer park where he grew up. "So," Howard says, smiling awkwardly at Joe, who is rubbing his head, "you're going to listen to me."

"Whatever," Joe mutters.

Rain starts to fall as they resume pushing for the final few feet. Once inside, as the Camaro coasts toward the wall, Porsche slams on the brake pedal and all three of them career chest first into the back of the car.

Porsche hears the banging and glances up to see the aftermath in the rearview mirror and laughs.

"Very fucking funny," Brandy yells, standing up, shaking her jammed wrists.

"It's okay," Howard says. "Thanks for driving."

"Yeah, 'cause driving was, like, really the hard part," Joe says.

"What did I say about being a smart-ass, Joe?" Brandy says, wagging a finger.

"You couldn't do it," Porsche says to Joe, stepping out of the car, wearing tight jeans, Roxy boots, and a red sweater.

"Yeah, I could."

"Shut up, you're ten."

"You shut up. You're only twelve."

"Shut up all of you," Howard says.

He takes a long breath, surveys the space. Now that it is raining he notices that thin streams of rainwater are squeezing through and gathering on the rafters, pooling into drops that gravity tugs down.

"It's leaking in here," Porsche says.

"Yes," Howard says to Porsche, as if she just illuminated the situation. "You're right."

"Yes," Brandy echoes. "I forgot about that."

"Joe," Howard says.

"Yeah?"

"I'm going to have a project for you."

Brandy stares at Howard until it dawns on her. "You're not putting him on the roof?"

"It's safest. He's the lightest."

"I can do it, Mom."

"This should be funny," Porsche says.

Rain increasing, Joe climbs up the ladder and then crawls onto the roof. As he stands he realizes he likes being up here, likes the view, likes being away from everyone. Just beyond the barn is a creek that separates their property from the family who live south of them, and he has never seen the creek from this angle. The water is dark except in patches where it narrows and froths over rocks. On the other side of the creek are a few houses spaced far apart and long strips of pastures, mostly undeveloped land. Beyond that, snowcapped Mount Rainier, shrouded in clouds, dominates the horizon.

"What are you doing?" Howard yells up. "How many?"

Joe's assignment is to identify and estimate the number of roof shingles that are missing or broken.

"There's a lot," is the first thing he reports back.

He steps toward a particularly damaged area and his boot slips on a patch of moss and *whoooosh,* he's on his back and sliding down the roof fast and suddenly he's airborne, feet first, and headed toward the ground, as though launched from a very long and high slide. He lands on his feet and then his butt and hands, mud kicking up into the air.

"Fuccccccck." He grabs his ankle and begins rolling around on the ground swearing.

Brandy and Howard are quickly upon him, trying to help without much effect, while Porsche stands there impressed.

"Wow," she says to nobody in particular. "Awesome."

"You okay, honey?" Brandy keeps asking in a rapid-fire voice. "You okay, honey, you okay?"

Joe just keeps swearing and rolling around, caking himself with mud. "Fuck, fuck, fuck, stupid fucking barn." His yelling sets a dog off in the distance.

"Can you walk it off?"

Joe continues to carry on, not hearing this.

"We have to take him to the hospital," Brandy says, kneeling helplessly.

"No." Howard grabs Joe's leg, runs a hand over the calf and ankle. "He's fine. Nothing's broken."

"How do you know? You don't know."

Howard stands, and lifts Brandy up to her feet while Joe continues to moan. "Here's the thing," he explains. "You take him to a hospital, and they're going to ask questions, get CPS involved, call you a shitty mother."

"Why, what did I do?"

"It's going to be a whole fucking horrible scene. You want to lose your kids?"

"I didn't do anything wrong!"

"They don't care. Kid comes in injured, there's a whole investigation. You still scamming welfare?"

"Yeah, but—"

"They'll look into everything. We can't take him to a hospital. A private doctor would be okay, a local doctor. Who won't call fucking CPS."

"Doctors don't work on weekends."

"So you can take him in later, if necessary."

"What's he do until then?" Brandy goes back to her knees, leans over her child helplessly. He has curled up and his profanity has subsided into quiet tears. "He's really hurt," she says, a long-dormant maternal instinct stirring slightly.

"I have plenty of Vicodin," Howard says. "Mostly in my storage unit. He can have some. Like I said, we're a family now."

"You have Vicodin? Any OxyContin?"

TWELVE

Using Porsche as his mechanic's assistant, focused from the remaining meth he does not share with Brandy, Howard spends almost an hour in the barn reconstructing and reinstalling the carburetor, fully engaged with the task at hand, his universe reduced to a simple, solvable puzzle.

"Start it up," he says to Porsche.

He stands by the open hood while she slides into the driver's seat.

"Now?"

"Now."

She turns the key and the old Camaro's 305-cubic-inch V-8 cranks up with an unsteady rumble.

"Wow!" Howard yells, surprised. "Okay. Go ahead and turn it off."

"Sounds better," she says after shutting it down. Though she affects a bored attitude, she enjoys the fact that they accomplished something. "It really does."

"Yep. Now go check on your mom and Joe, then clean up and change. I'll pick you up in the driveway."

"Yeah?"

"We've got errands to run."

After Porsche rushes off, Howard turns his last baggie of meth inside out and snorts the residue, running his nose across the plastic, sucking back and forth until there is absolutely nothing more to be consumed. He then washes his hands in the gasoline he used to clean the carburetor, takes off his dirty sweatshirt from over his Wells Fargo Bank T-shirt. He likes the stagecoach logo.

Backing the Camaro out of the barn, he pulls a Y turn in the dirt and grass, then drives through the open gate and idles in front of the house, proud to be mobile.

Porsche emerges from the front door wearing the same tight jeans, a thigh-length faux-fur coat that hangs open, a black studded choker, lipstick, and a short white shirt that leaves her midriff exposed. Howard is not sure exactly when twelve-year-old girls starting dressing like hookers, but he likes the trend.

"Where are we going?" she asks as she climbs into the passenger's seat.

"We have to get Joe some medicine."

"Mom's giving him beer, so he likes that."

"Places to go," Howard says, tapping his hands on the steering wheel, "things to do."

Porsche senses that he wants her to be all curious and beg for information, and so she just shrugs indifferently.

"So, you're twelve now?" he asks, staying within the speed limit.

"Thirteen in January."

"What do you want to be when you're older?"

"Famous."

"Okay. How?"

"I was kidding. *Jesus*." She slouches farther back, stomach exposed. "I don't know what I want to do."

"Most people lack ambition."

"Including me, I guess."

"It's never too early to have goals."

Porsche shrugs and holds up her thumbs and forefingers in a W and says, "What*ever*."

Howard is both annoyed and aroused by her immaturity.

Almost missing a red light, he stops at the last second, slamming the brakes.

"Whoa, speed racer," she says.

"You can always walk."

"What. Ever."

"So . . . what do you and your girlfriends do for fun?" he asks, ignoring her petulance, taking a free right turn because he does not like waiting for lights.

"Party."

"Yeah? Who with?"

"Guys from the high school mostly."

Jealousy seizes Howard as he thinks of the pimply-faced adolescent boys who no doubt do not appreciate their time of good opportunity.

"You drink?"

"Of course. Everybody does. Well, not everybody, but everybody I hang out with."

"Drugs?"

"Yeah."

"Like?"

"Mushrooms, when we can find 'em. Weed, of course. Ecstasy. Some girls like meth."

"You?"

"What?"

"You like meth?"

"Of course."

"You're a little young for meth," he says, testing.

"I know plenty of girls my age who use it."

"Yeah?"

"It helps you stay skinny and stuff."

"Yeah, that's true."

"And Vicodin," she adds, putting the hint out there. "Sometimes that's going around. I like it."

Sitting up and bringing the jacket in around herself, Porsche pulls a pack of Marlboro Lights from her pocket. She glances at Howard as she pushes in the car lighter.

"Your mom lets you smoke?"

"Just not in the house."

She turns on the radio, dials in KNDD at the far right of the dial, cranks it up.

"Who's this?" Howard asks.

"The Strokes. Preppy East Coast guys, but I like them anyway."

"*I wanna steal your innocence, to me my life doesn't make no sense . . .*"

"Catchy tune," he says.

"'Barely Legal.'"

"What?"

"That's the song title."

Howard catches her coy smile out of the corner of his eye and wonders if she is teasing him or if he is imagining this.

After a couple more songs—tunes Porsche knows and he does not—they pull into a Shurgard storage facility in Lakewood. They drive past several orange and white garage-sized units and stop at the back.

Howard hops out of the car and crosses to the combination lock hanging on the door latch. He pulls a piece of paper from his wallet and reads the combination, lips moving. Twice before he used a hacksaw on the locks because he could not remember the combination, but he does not want to switch to a standard padlock because of the fear of being caught with the key.

Porsche steps up behind him and watches as he opens the door. Stacks of junk come into view: cardboard boxes, plastic milk crates, porno magazines, blue tarps, full green garbage bags, propane tanks, a pinball machine, and an ATM machine with a gold and red logo and lettering that matches Howard's Wells Fargo Bank T-shirt.

Her nose crinkles as she smells ammonia. "Yuck."

"What?"

"That smell."

"Cleaning fluids," he says automatically, though there is no reason to lie other than habit.

He tries to open the trunk of the car with the ignition key, but it will not turn. He keeps trying until the key starts to bend.

"Mom lost the trunk key a long time ago."

"How do you get into the trunk?"

"We don't."

"You don't?" He shakes his head. "Okay, open the passenger door and slide the seat forward."

Porsche does and he wheels the ATM machine over from the storage unit and lifts it up and shoves it onto the back seat of the car, the top edge of the machine catching on the aging vinyl and ripping a gash, which stops their progress. Howard then manhandles the machine into place.

"You ever work as a baggage handler?" Porsche asks.

Howard ignores her and returns into the unit, rummages through a cardboard box.

"Bingo," he says.

Porsche observes closely as he shoves two prescription pill bottles into his pocket, then holds a third bottle up. He walks toward her until the label is inches from her face.

VICODIN, it says, prescribed to Bret E. Ellis.

"Who's Bret Ellis?" Porsche asks.

"Me, for about a year." This was after he read *American Pyscho*, his all-time favorite novel, and one of the very few he has read to the end.

He taps one pill out and holds it up with two fingers like a jewel. Porsche wants to grab for it, but resists the temptation.

"Want one?" he asks.

She shrugs, then nods and holds out her hand. He starts to hand it to her, then pulls it back, grinning.

"Hey!"

"We'll get something to wash it down with," he says. "Vicodin doesn't really work without booze."

Howard closes up the unit, and they drive away, the ATM machine rattling in the back seat. They stop at a 7-Eleven and pull into the corner of the lot. He leaves the engine running.

"Do you have fake ID?"

"No."

"Well," he says, handing her a twenty, "go in and try to buy cigarettes and beer and see what happens."

"I'll tell you what will happen. Nothing."

"Try it."

As she enters the store, the middle-aged male clerk's eyes follow her. Howard meanwhile unloads the ATM machine, which he wheels up against a wall near the front entrance, just out of the sight line of the clerk. He flips a switch in back and activates the modified computer, which lights up like the real thing.

Shortly after he finishes, Porsche emerges from the store empty-handed. She joins Howard who is waiting in the car with the engine still running.

"You're not as hot as you thought, are you?"

"I'm twelve."

"Give me back the money."

Porsche hands him back the twenty, notices the ATM machine on the sidewalk against the store wall.

"Hey," she says. "What's up with that?"

"Stay here and watch."

Howard buys a pack of Kools, a six-pack of Mike's Hard Lemonade, a can of Mountain Dew, and copies of *People* and *Penthouse* magazines. He returns to the car and hands the lemonade to Porsche. They wash down Vicodins with the malt liquor and light cigarettes and wait.

"Nothing's happening," she says.

"Patience, hon."

Howard picks up the *Penthouse* magazine, quickly finds the centerfold.

Porsche turns the radio back on, tunes in KEXP, "member-supported radio," which plays everything from alternative rock to country. She nods along to the Killers.

After a few minutes a man pulls up in a massive new pickup truck and steps up to the machine and puts his card into the intake slot. *English or Spanish* flashes up on the screen, followed by a command to enter his PIN number.

After he puts in his PIN number, the screen flashes, *Sorry, unable to process at this time. Please contact your financial institution.*

"Now we have his ATM card and his PIN number," Howard explains to Porsche as the man futilely continues to push buttons.

"Where did you get it, the machine?"

"I got it in trade for some stuff. It's paid for itself many times over."

"Can you get them on, like, eBay?"

"I don't think so. You need to know people."

"You know people?"

"I know people."

They continue waiting and watching, turning on the windshield wipers when sheets of rain begin falling across the parking lot. A second victim, a woman driving an old Honda, follows the same steps to disappointment as the previous mark. Porsche shakes her head and laughs.

"This is awesome."

"Sometimes it's a good thing that I live my life surrounded by morons."

Two more victims later, too jittery to sit any longer, Howard wheels the machine back to the car and loads it into the back seat after removing the ATM cards and the PIN log.

They drive to various ATMs and Howard makes the maximum withdrawal from each, one card per ATM. There is no reason he cannot use all four cards in one machine, but he habitually spreads out his hits on the theory that he wants his trail to be as difficult as possible to follow. Cops, he believes, are mostly lazy and overwhelmed and chase the incompetent criminals, the ones who are easiest to catch.

As he is heading south on Pacific Avenue, counting the loot in his head, he becomes careless and exceeds the speed limit. Suddenly a Tacoma Police car lights up its wig-wags behind them.

"Fuck me," Howard says, startling Porsche.

"What?"

There's a single burst from the siren as the patrol car pulls closer.

"Hold on."

His foot presses down on the pedal and he swings out into the left lane. He accelerates and cuts between traffic, putting distance between himself and the patrol car. One of the things Howard likes about Tacoma, and the reason he executes most of his scams in the city, is that the police department has a no-pursuit policy.

At the first intersection he makes a crazily dangerous left turn through oncoming traffic, laughing at the honks, knowing the patrol car cannot follow. Two reckless turns later, he loses the officer.

"Bonnie and Clyde without killing anyone," he says to Porsche, reaching into his pocket and removing five twenties, which he drops onto her lap.

"Thanks."

"Let's keep this adventure to ourselves."

Porsche nods and pockets the money with no hesitation, buzzed from the Hard Lemonade and the Vicodin and the adrenaline of it all.

"I'm going to let you hold some of goodies here." He hands her three Vicodins as they pull up in front of her mother's house. "Give a couple to your brother if he needs them. One-half at a time. And it's okay if you have one yourself, but not more than one."

Howard feels confident he can parlay the day's activities into sex, a plan much like when he used to take girls to the Puyallup Fair and the thrill of the rides operated as foreplay, but he does not sense that the time is right yet.

"I'll be back later," he says.

"Where are you going?" Porsche asks, her affectation of indifference completely dropped.

"I need money for my project. It takes money to make money."

In Howard's experience girls like ambition, even in their bad boys. Though he did not graduate from high school, has never held down a job, and treats women shoddily, he has always, as he likes to put it, *done well with the ladies.*

Inside a motel room just off the freeway, four tweekers make their way in the world by sifting through trash and mail. Their dingy nicotine-stained room with closed curtains is filled with garbage bags, meth pipes, mirrors and razors, butts on the floor, empty baggies with white residue, Scotch tape, an X-acto knife, a Dell computer, a Hewlett-Packard 620C printer, and a GBC 40 laminator, the high-tech tool of choice for identity thieves.

One stunningly thin blond woman, who usually works as a prostitute, sits cross-legged and methodically tapes together shredded credit card bills from out of a garbage bag. She finds the matching puzzle pieces of the long strips next to each other usually, often tangled together.

Beside her is a midget rummaging through a vinyl gym bag of stolen mail, separating out the potentially useful items into a cardboard box, his speedy little hands moving like a squirrel's. He is wearing a University of Puget Sound T-shirt that says LOGGERS across the front.

Both of them only vaguely know the man who is paying them, but they know what they need to know: Howard pays in high quality Nazi meth and he has been delivering regularly. He takes the information, prints out licenses and checks, lays out the lines, fills the pipes, and leaves. High as they are, it still occurs to them that if there is a bust, they will likely take the rap. However, they care only in the most abstract sense of the word.

People will stress endlessly and lose hundreds of hours of their lives trying to clean up the damage from the theft of their identity, but the only consequences the tweekers consider are the minimal sentences they will face if caught. They know their plea bargains will probably not require jail time, the fines will go unpaid, and the government will pay for their attorneys. Identity thieves come to Pierce County from all over the state because it is well known that the prosecutors and the cops are snowed under with cases.

When there is a knock on the door followed by, "Police, warrant," and seconds later the door is kicked in and four Fife police officers enter in a clattering rush and take positions with their weapons drawn, it is not a big shock or upset for the tweekers.

"Hands the fuck up!"

"Police!"

The midget and the blond prostitute both raise their hands, and though they are shaking it is from the meth rather than fear. They are not quite grasping the situation. Still, they remember their patron's advice—don't talk except to say you want a lawyer.

Wyatt arrives in the parking lot, called out by the Fife detective he tipped off based on Marvin's information. The blonde and the midget sit in the backs of separate patrol cars as the scene is processed.

Barely peeking up over the bottom of the window are the midget's eyes, staring at Wyatt, who is standing in the parking lot with the detective. The riffraff has temporarily cleared out of the area.

"The midget keeps looking over here," Wyatt says.

"He lawyered up."

"No sign of Howard?"

"Well, there are signs of somebody; these tweekers weren't working alone."

"Any latents?"

"Unlikely."

"Any cigarette butts, anything we can pull DNA from?"

"You fucking kidding? This ain't *CSI*."

Wyatt nods, understanding. DNA testing is expensive and time-consuming and only used on homicide cases, rapes, and television.

"I should talk to the midget," he says.

"I told you, he lawyered up."

"Guess it won't be admissible, then."

Wyatt turns and approaches the patrol car where the midget sits in back. "Hello," Wyatt says, opening the door of the car and lowering himself onto his haunches next to a rain puddle in the uneven concrete.

"You busted me before." The midget's voice is deep.

"Yeah, a lab in Buckley."

"You let me go."

"Yep." Wyatt cannot remember why exactly, except that he probably did not make the midget to be one of the ringleaders, or maybe the midget gave him information. "I see you haven't been staying out of trouble."

"It's harder than it sounds."

"Whose operation was this?"

"Not mine."

"Not hers, either?"

"No. She's brain-dead."

The midget keeps jerking around, his stubby legs kicking up involuntarily, head bobbing, face twitching, and though Wyatt has seen all these meth tics before, they are especially disconcerting in a midget.

"So this was Howard's operation," he says.

"Is that his name? He never told us his name."

"Did the woman with you know him at all?"

"No."

"How did you end up in business with him?"

"A friend of mine."

"Who's your friend?"

"I don't know his name."

Wyatt knows that the midget, like most suspects, has talking parameters he will have to work around. Still, the midget strikes Wyatt as a survivor, someone who might know enough to pull his hand out of the coconut.

"What did Howard look like?"

"Short, skinny, muscular."

Wyatt is not sure what short means in the eyes of a midget. "How short?"

"Five-foot-five, I guess."

"White?"

"Yeah."

"What kind of complexion?"

"Bad."

"Hair?"

"Long, blond. Goatee kinda."

"Tats?"

"Swastika on his forearm, I think."

"Which arm?"

"I don't remember."

"Anything else about him you remember?"

"He had good meth."

"Nazi or Red P?"

While there really is no discernible difference in the final product, tweekers generally think otherwise, and cooks often boast of their particular technique.

"Nazi," the midget says. "Pretty pure."

"Do you remember what kind of shoes he wore?"

"Boots. Cowboy boots."

"Color?"

"Black."

"Thanks." Wyatt rises, starts to close the car door.

"Can you get me out of this?"

"Sorry."

"Next time, maybe."

"Maybe."

Back in the motel room, the gloved detective is bagging up items that might have latent fingerprints—Mountain Dew cans, an ashtray, a meth pipe—when Wyatt enters. This is not something the small-town detective would normally bother with on a minor case, but he knows about Wyatt's obsession with Howard and can relate. Almost all officers have come across the one bad guy who crawls under their skin.

"Thanks," Wyatt says.

"Is this Howard's work?"

"Not absolutely sure." Just then Wyatt notices a crumpled Starbucks cup lying on its side next to the computer, logo up. "But sure enough."

Two of the wooden booths at the downtown Swiss Pub are marked with plaques reserving them for local congressmen Adam Smith and Norm Dicks. The reserved status is honorary and not taken literally by anyone and the booths are often filled with drinkers who have no idea who their congressmen are and do not care, except to believe strongly that they should be doing more for Pierce County and Tacoma.

In 1993 the Swiss Hall was just another boarded-up downtown building in an area populated by drug dealers, addicts, vagrants, and the occasional hooker. Gayle, a chef, and Bob, and Jack, bartenders from Engine House #9, leased the building from the University of Washington. They tore the faux-wood paneling off the brick walls, opened up the pressed-tin ceiling, cleaned the concrete floors, polished the mahogany bar, and opened for business.

Quickly the Swiss became a beacon amid downtown dilapidation, a casual hangout for politicians, prosecutors, defense lawyers, and a diverse crowd of young and old locals that vary with the bands. Tacoman Dale Chihuly, jazzed by the idea of a cool bar in his 'hood, donated half a million dollars' worth of glass art: eight spindly and shiny pieces that sit on a brightly lit ridge behind the bar just above the beer taps and bottles.

Mike and his date, June, a teacher and English lit PhD candidate with short hair, cat-eye glasses, and excellent cheekbones, are here early to have dinner before the cover band, the Retros, fills the club with songs by the Cure, Depeche Mode, Psychedelic Furs, the Bangles, the Smiths, and all the rest that send Mike into nostalgic reverie.

When he is on a date that is going well, he feels he might live a long time and does not worry about accepting death. June and he have been going out for two months and she usually has that effect on him.

He is enjoying a house specialty, pan-fried oysters, in the Adam Smith booth, listening to June talk about her comparative literature paper on Kurt Vonnegut and Jacqueline Susann and their concurrently best-selling novels, when his cell phone rings.

Wyatt James comes up on the LCD screen.

"Business," Mike says to June. "Excuse me."

"No problem," June says good-naturedly, setting down her salad fork and reaching for her scotch on the rocks.

"What's up, Wyatt?"

"Marvin's tip was good. Busted some of Howard's tweeker thieves in a motel room with lots of stolen mail."

"And Howard?"

"Missed him."

"Anyone talk?"

"Midget talked, gave me a description of the ringleader that pretty much matched Howard."

"Midget, did you say?"

Mike looks over at his date, who is holding up her glass and wiping off a smudge.

"Yeah," Wyatt continues, "he was working for Howard, though he didn't know he was working for Howard."

"Sounds like we should discuss this next week?"

"What are you doing?"

"Trying to have a life."

"Are you on a date?"

"Yes."

"So why did you pick it up?"

"I thought it might be important."

"You made a mistake."

"Clearly."

"I want the go-ahead to put Marvin on contract. He's proven his reliability, chief."

"Let's talk about this later, okay?"

"How's your date going?"

"Very well," Mike says, smiling at her, "if I don't continue this conversation much longer."

"Best line from *Doctor Zhivago*?"

"'The personal life is dead.'"

June looks up. "*Doctor Zhivago*," she mouths to him.

"Yes," Mike says to June, impressed.

"Who are you with," Wyatt asks. "June?"

"It's Wyatt," Mike says to her. "Good night, Wyatt."

June's cell phone rings with a chime similar to Mike's phone and she answers it, shrugging apologetically.

"I can't decide if I miss dating or not," Wyatt says. "Is it cool? Not knowing whether or not she is going to sleep with you tonight, wondering what comes next?"

"Say hi to Suki for me."

"I'm serious about putting Marvin on contract."

"Good night."

Mike hangs up. June follows suit a moment later.

"My friend lost her Prozac," she explains.

"Prozac, very old-school."

"Are you on Prozac, or lithium, or Klonopin, or . . . *anything?*"

"No."

"Me neither." She smiles. "Wow."

Sound checks float in from the other room, including the

opening riff from "Don't You (Forget About Me)," which causes them both to smile in recognition.

"Which version of 'Pretty in Pink' do you prefer?" June asks, hand moving lightly to her cheek. "The *Talk, Talk, Talk* recording, or the movie soundtrack?"

"*Talk, Talk, Talk.* You?"

"The same." June nods. "Do you own the CD?"

"Yes. You?"

"I have both, even though soundtracks disrupt my CD organization. Have you heard of Wreckless Eric?"

"'Whole Wide World.'"

"Right." She smiles. "Do you have any of his CDs?"

"*Bungalow Hi* and *Greatest Stiffs.*"

"Do you put him under W or E? He's a person, not a band, so he should be listed by his last name, but what's his last name? Eric's his first name, right? And Wreckless isn't a name at all, it's an adjective."

"That's a good point," Mike says after a pause. "I wrestled with that, too, and I decided to treat him like a band and put him under W."

"That's a reasonable solution," June says. "But I think I might just say fuck it and switch to an iPod."

"iPods are a relatively safe addiction."

Mike's cell phone rings again and they look at each other for a beat, then simultaneously turn off their phones.

Frustrated with Howard's elusiveness, frustrated with Mike's nonchalance, frustrated that he comes home alone on a Saturday though he has a girlfriend, Wyatt resorts to a reliable tonic: *The Godfather* on DVD. He has all three parts, but the first remains his favorite.

He sips a Cabernet on the couch as the movie begins with Bonasera, the mortician, in the Godfather's dark study, reporting that his daughter was beaten in an attempted rape.

"I went to the police, like a good American. These two boys were brought to trial. The judge sentenced them to three years in prison—suspended sentence. Suspended sentence! They went free that very day! I stood in the courtroom like a fool. And those two bastards, they smiled at me. Then I said to my wife, for justice, we must go to Don Corleone."

Before Marlon Brando can make things right, Wyatt's cell phone rings. He picks up only because it is Suki.

"Can you come get me?" she asks, her voice unusually pleading, music pounding in the background. "I'm at the club and I didn't drive."

"You okay?"

"Just please come get me."

Wyatt drives his own vehicle, a navy-blue Jeep Wrangler with a removable hardtop, to Foxes in Parkland, just north of Pacific Lutheran University. He parks beneath a tall pole with a weathered marquee advertising FULL NUDE DANCING, OPEN UNTIL 3:00 A.M.

Outside the unmarked front door of a one-story building

stands a bulky man in a white jumpsuit. He acts as a bouncer and an escort for the girls—walking them to their cars when their shifts are over. Suki always tips him, ending her night "as a tipper rather than a tippee."

Wyatt nods at the doorman and steps into the noise and darkness of the club, pausing to let his eyes adjust. At the front cash register he tells the assistant manager why he is here.

"Your name?"

"Wyatt James."

Quickly the assistant manager registers that Wyatt is probably a cop—it is part of his job to know these things. More than once the Pierce County Sheriff's Department has visited Foxes with vice operations, citing dancers for violations of the generally ignored ten-foot rule.

Lynnwood police, in Snowhomish County, more hands-on, bought "happy endings" for officers in a recent massage parlor sting. The prosecutor on the case, Mark Roe, dismissed the prostitution charges because of the investigative tactics and the media attention.

Strip clubs and massage parlors, meanwhile, meet the challenge by employing people with an eye for law enforcement.

"I'll get her right away, Detective," the assistant manager says to Wyatt with an obsequious smile.

Wyatt does not appreciate the familiarity.

Velvet Revolver plays through a sound system heavily laced with bass, and the thumping music and the darkness broken up by flashing lights disorient Wyatt as he scans the room.

There are three half-circle stages, each stage stretching out from a different wall. All the stages are lit with black lights and Fresnel gels. Two of the dancers are totally naked, their outfits strewn across the stages. The third one is on her back, legs together in the air, her bottoms momentarily tangling on her stiletto heels as she attempts to slide them off.

Closest to the stages are tables and chairs filled by young men who are there to watch the stage show. Beyond the tables are long couches where the men who want dances lurk. These are the men, generally older, who want to talk to the girls. They use the dancers as therapists and relationship counselors. Sometimes the men ask them out, offer to take them away from all this.

Leaning against the deejay booth is a pretty Filipina girl in pink lingerie, smoking. She wears a white orchid in her hair and Wyatt recognizes her as Suki's friend "Duchess," real name: Alexis. She and Suki belong to the same book club.

Beyond the deejay booth is the backstage door and a few moments after the assistant manager goes in, Suki comes out. She quickly crosses the club, carrying a black gym bag and wearing a tan cardigan over a white blouse and dark thrift-store skirt.

"Thanks," she says, taking his hand and not slowing down a step in her march out.

Not until they are in his Jeep and driving on the freeway does she ask a question. "When does someone become famous enough so that a murder is an assassination?"

"I don't think there's a bright-line standard."

"I can't take it there anymore," she says, putting on her seat-belt. "No more pornglish for me. *Je ne parle pas pornglish.*"

"Good."

"I quit."

"I figured."

"And I didn't want to wait around for Alexis."

"Since you quit midshift?"

"Right."

He wants to know why, but knows she will not talk about the details until she has mulled it over for a while. Like him, she does not easily give things up about herself.

She turns to him. "Are you glad?"

"Yes."

"I'll just work more hours at the coffee shop, at least until I go back to school."

"Good plan."

Wyatt turns the wipers on and the defroster up as pellets of rain start to smack against the windshield.

"I would have just taken a taxi," Suki says, "but I didn't do a single dance tonight. Sometimes you just hit a breaking point, you know?"

"I know."

"I was reading an interview with David Lynch, and he said there comes a time in most people's lives when they quit banging their head against the walls and become a seeker."

"That guy's a freak. He makes a good living at it, though."

"I'm going to be broke now."

Wyatt shrugs. "Money's not that important."

"People who grew up with plenty of it always say that. I didn't grow up with any, so it's important to me."

"It's not that important as long as you have a roof and food."

"Yeah, well, I'll have your roof." She smiles. "And I guess you'll be buying dinner more often."

Wyatt nods. "Subway will be getting lots of our business."

"You wanted me to quit, didn't you?"

"Of course."

"Why didn't you just say so?"

"It's better this way."

"That's not why, not because it's 'better.' You didn't say so because you thought that if you asked me to quit it would mean something, like asking me to quit would mean you were making a commitment or something."

Wyatt recognizes this as true, so he does not reply.

"We'll see how you adjust to having me around more," Suki says, lightening up as they put more distance between themselves and Foxes. "Let's do something now, like go to a movie, stop at a Starbucks, something normal people do on Saturdays."

COLORS

Joe's ankle, purple and yellow, is swollen to almost twice its normal size. His foot is propped up on a pillow and bread bags full of melting ice are wrapped around the contusion.

"The swelling's gone down some," Howard says, feeling good from a meth recharge.

"Not fucking much," Joe says, staring at the freakish abnormality his ankle has become.

"The pain better?"

At this the boy nods gratefully.

"Your sister took care of you?"

"Yeah."

"Good girl."

Howard reaches into his pocket and pulls out a Vicodin and sets the pill between a CD player and an empty Mountain Dew can on the nightstand.

"Take that when you need it. But not before."

"Thanks."

"You know where I've been?"

"No."

"Porsche didn't tell you?"

"No."

She's a good one.

Joe is anxious for Howard to leave so he can pop the Vicodin. He is not sure why he is waiting, but thinks he should.

"Don't go out in the barn," Howard says, out of nowhere.

"The barn?"

"Yeah, it's my private workshop."

Suddenly it occurs to Howard that telling a boy not to do something is tantamount to daring him.

"Never mind," Howard adds, as though this will negate the dare.

"What?"

"Nothing." Howard is confusing himself. "I'll see you in a day or two."

"Should you leave more pills with me?"

"I'll leave them with Porsche."

"Okay. Thanks."

"No prob. We're a family now."

As Howard exits, stepping over the clothes, the shoes, and the CDs by rappers named 2Pac, 50cent, Eminem, Snoop Dogg, and Ludacris—not a properly spelled word in sight—he notices red shoelaces on a pair of Doc Martens.

"Joe?"

"Yeah?"

"Do you know what red shoelaces mean?"

"Yeah."

"What?"

"It means you've beat up someone of an inferior race. Enough to make them bleed."

This, Howard knows, is correct.

"How old are you?"

"Almost eleven."

"Ten."

"Don't worry, I earned them."

"Yeah? Who did you beat up?"

"Mexican kid."

"That's fucking stupid."

"Why?"

"Because Mexicans have big brothers and cousins and they could kick your ass bad."

These words do not seem strong enough to Howard, and he cannot seem to find words that do, so he walks back to Joe and punches him in the side of his head at half speed, leaving no mark but what he hopes will be a lasting impression.

Joe's mouth flops open from the impact and surprise.

"You're a tough kid, I like that. But I don't want to see you get your ass killed. So watch it, okay?"

Joe is confused because Howard seems to actually care.

"Are the white kids at school listening to that rap crap?"

"Yeah."

"What's up with that?"

"I dunno."

"Joe, you seem a little confused. You can't wear red shoelaces and listen to Negroes."

"Eminem is white."

"You're missing the fucking . . . point." Howard, however, has not slept in almost three days and he has lost the point himself and so cannot share it with Joe. "Just fucking . . . be tough, use your head, don't take any wooden nickels, okay?" Howard turns and heads into the hallway, muttering.

Shortening the amount of time between doses, Howard stays focused enough to go on a shopping spree, leaving shredded credit histories in his wake. In seventy sleepless hours he prepares the barn for business.

Each corner of the barn has a video camera, and two more cameras are mounted on the fence where the dirt driveway meets the road. All the cameras are wireless, and there are two television monitors in the house, another in the barn.

Electronics in the barn are powered by thick extension cords running over a hundred feet back to the house. Several lighter-duty extension cords snake out from surge protectors, supplying electricity to two blenders, two extra-large pancake griddles, a refrigerator, and four sets of double fluorescent lights in white metal shields nailed crudely to the walls of the barn.

The blenders and the griddles are on top of the workbench, along with multiple cans of HEET, Coleman fuel, liquid drain opener, coffee filters, funnels, a bag of rock salt, two propane tanks full of anhydrous ammonia, and numerous mason jars. In the drawers of the workbench are dozens of lithium batteries.

On the floor between the car and the bench are two crude HCL generators, gas cans with rubber stoppers in place of the cap and tubes hanging out. Next to these is a freezer for converting the meth powder to crystal for the ice freaks. Howard recognizes there is no chemical difference—ice is just a crystallized form of methamphetamine—but some users believe devoutly in the purity of ice and Howard, like Nordstrom's, recognizes that the customer is always right.

With this lab Howard plans to make two batches at a time, working on a phase of batch two while he waits for a phase of batch one to complete, thereby staying in motion constantly and producing significant quantities. No more dealing in penny-ante teeners, he will market $600 ounces cut with MSM, a dietary supplement for horses, pounds of powder for around $5,000, and pounds of ice in the $9,000 neighborhood, depending on market fluctuations. He is ready to go head-to-head with the Mexicans who have to hustle their product across the border.

"Be patriotic," he tells customers, "buy American."

All he needs to kick-start his meth factory is pseudo-ephedrine, which is becoming increasingly difficult to obtain with local runners.

Adapting, Howard sets up a six-pound pseudo purchase with a Canadian who lives in Bellingham. He has heard that terrorists are moving into the pseudo business, supplementing their oil and poppy field profits, but business is business.

Howard and the Canadian agree to meet in Seattle in the parking lot of the downtown Déjà Vu, the only landmark business that comes to mind. Because it is outside of Pierce County, Howard expects it is less likely to be a setup. Local agencies generally do not like to reach outside their jurisdictions.

Or so he tries to persuade himself as the paranoia kicks in and he smokes a quick bowl to take the edge off the wait, parked with the trunk against the brick wall of Déjà Vu. He inhales deeply as he studies the parking lot and First Avenue through the drizzle-spotted windows. On his right is a large gray van with no windows, *a rape van*, as they are known in Pierce County.

Howard is using a client's car, the Firebird of the kid who was arrested. Howard gave the kid's girlfriend the money to get the car out of impound. He did not want to use Brandy's, as it could be tracked back to her. The level of his paranoia, and therefore the extent of his security precautions, varies drastically from day to day, hour to hour, minute to minute.

Just as the smoky rush of invincibility kicks in from his lungs to his brain and down to his wiggling feet, Howard sees the Canadian's silver Lincoln Navigator pull into the lot. Surprisingly quick, the monster SUV maneuvers over and pulls into the spot on Howard's left. Howard and the Canadian have only met once, in the Pierce County Jail where the Canadian had a short stay, but they have mutual acquaintances in the drug world.

They step out of their vehicles and shake hands and they are remarkably similar physically: two wiry guys with goatees and long unwashed hair. The Canadian is shorter.

"Nice sled," Howard says.

"Too bad business isn't better."

"Yeah, they've clamped down on Sudafed and all the over-the-counter pseudo."

"Fuckin' politicians."

"Goddamn government."

They are chattering rapidly, twitching and grinding teeth and looking all around, their heads rotating like geese.

"So let's do it," Howard says, anxious to get back to the barn for cooking.

The Canadian swings the heavy passenger door of the Navigator open and he reaches behind the front seat and pulls out a black duffel bag with a white Nike swoosh across both sides.

"Six American pounds," he says.

Howard nods and hands him a Stadium Thriftway grocery bag with thirty-five hundred dollars. This takes a while for the Canadian to count out, as it is mostly in twenties from ATM machines.

"It's all there," Howard says.

The Canadian quits counting and stashes the money in the SUV, not because he trusts Howard, but because he already lost count twice and does not feel like trying a third time. He expects he will see Howard again.

"I'll call you," Howard says as he climbs into his car, setting the duffel bag on the passenger's seat.

As the Canadian walks into Déjà Vu, Howard pulls out onto First Avenue and drives south past the Pike Place Market and the ShowBox Theater, oblivious to the numerous pedestrians and the neon of the city reflecting off the wet cement, tunnel vision taking hold. He is grateful the rain has let up because windshield wipers can sometimes drive him batty.

On the freeway he drives at exactly fifty-five miles per hour until he's past Tacoma and off 512 and onto Pacific Avenue and the Mountain Highway. Clenching his sweaty hands on the wheel, he rolls down the window and enjoys the air as he starts to speed up.

He is only a few miles from home, tailgating a pickup truck, when suddenly an old Dodge Dart comes fishtailing around a corner of the wet road and the pickup's red brake lights flash and he locks his brakes just as he hears the smoking screech of brakes from the other vehicles.

Seconds later the Dart and the pickup truck clip head-on into each other and the Dart spins off into the ditch, radiator steam jetting out from under the hood. The pickup spins and ends up sideways across the road. Howard's foot is frozen on the floor and his eyes close as the Firebird is about to slam into the side of the pickup, but the impact is not as severe as he expects.

Opening his eyes, heart pounding madly, Howard appraises the scene. First he notices an overpowering odor of ammonia, the odor of a mobile meth lab. In a shallow ditch the Dart sits crippled, hood bent, steaming. The pickup, completely blocking the road, has a badly damaged front corner, a quarter panel bent back onto a flat tire. On the side of the road are green garbage bags, broken mason jars, and a propane tank.

He steps out and checks the front of his car. Damage appears minimal—one broken headlight with wires hanging down helplessly.

The driver of the pickup stumbles out of the cab and Howard immediately recognizes him, a local tweeker.

"Wow," the tweeker says.

"Shit," says the driver of the Dart, who squeezes out of the passenger door, which opens only partially. Howard recognizes him as well, another local tweeker.

This is not a reunion Howard wants to be party to, especially when the police and the fire department make their appearance. He climbs back into the Firebird, backs up, and drives around the pickup on the open side of the road, trying to avoid the jars and broken glass.

Once clear, he speeds away from the scene as fast as he can, vaguely appreciating the poetic justice of almost being undone by tweekers he may have supplied. Only a couple miles from where he is about to turn onto Brandy's street, a Pierce County Sheriff's Jeep Cherokee drives past him toward the accident.

Maintain, maintain.

Deputy Newton remembers the Firebird with the gray primer hood from the previous encounter, and the broken headlight is an invitation for a stop even though his shift is done. He executes a quick U-turn and speeds up behind Howard and lights him up with the wig-wags.

"Fuck, fuck, shit." Howard pounds the wheel.

Flight, fight, or surrender thoughts ping-pong around his brain, but his first instinct is to push the gas pedal down. The Firebird jerks forward with a horrible rattle.

Deputy Newton sees the Firebird speed up and follows suit—*if they run, they're guilty.* Pierce County cops, unlike Tacoma's, still give chase. Adrenaline surges as he gains ground, closing fast.

Howard reaches over with his right hand and stuffs the duffel bag under the passenger seat as his left hand grips the steering wheel, the car shaking and swerving. Once the duffel bag is mostly out of sight, he slows down and pulls over, muttering to himself, *"Maintain, maintain."*

Because the chase was only a short burst, the deputy does not draw his weapon when he pulls up behind Howard. However, he does keep one hand on the butt of his Glock .40 as he approaches the driver's side of the car.

Howard pulls out a driver's license from his wallet—Lars Ulrich—and then rolls down his window.

"License, registration, and insurance, please."

"I'm just borrowing the car," Howard says as he hands over the license.

Deputy Newton looks back and forth from the license to Howard, and recognizes him as the passenger he had to release after their previous encounter. Howard makes the same connection a few seconds later.

Lars Ulrich sounds dimly familiar, but the deputy is twenty-one and not a Metallica fan and so the name is lost on him.

"Does the owner have registration or insurance, Mr. Ulrich?"

"Probably not." Howard smiles, hoping to impress the deputy with his honesty.

"I pulled you over because you have a headlight out."

"Sorry about that. I've been meaning to change it, or replace it. Put in a new one."

"Why did you try to elude me when I activated my lights?"

"I didn't, it wasn't a Felony Elude."

This use of the proper legal term arouses the deputy's suspicions, and the swastika tattoo on Howard's forearm does not help to dispel his misgivings.

"You sped up," the deputy says.

"It was an accident."

"An accident?"

"I accidentally pushed down on the gas pedal. I meant to push down on the brake."

"You sped up for nearly half a minute."

"I don't think it was that long."

"And you were swerving."

"I was swerving? You sure?"

"Yep."

"But I pulled over, though. When I saw you. As soon as I saw you. Here I am, see? Pulled over."

Deputy Newton recognizes that Howard is tweaking, but he has seen far worse and he doubts Howard would flunk field sobriety tests. Eyeing the interior, the deputy notices a Nike bag poking out from under the passenger's seat, and he figures this is what Howard was reaching for when he was leaning over during the pursuit.

"Are there any weapons in the bag?"

"Where?" Howard's head pivots back and forth quickly, sweat glistening.

Bingo, there's something in the bag.

"On the passenger floorboard."

"I don't know whose it is. Must be the guy whose car this is, I guess."

Howard compliments himself for using the kid's car.

"I saw you reaching over there when I was pulling you over."

"I was just adjusting things."

"What were you adjusting?"

Howard knows he should probably shut up, but he also thinks he can still talk himself out of this, and these thoughts collide and confuse him.

"Adjusting? What?"

"You were adjusting the bag?"

"I was, yeah, it was slipping around, so I pushed it back."

"Are there any weapons in the bag?"

"It was slipping out," Howard rambles on, "like onto my feet, causing problems, driving problems, and so I pushed it."

"It was under your seat?"

"Under my *feet*. It was . . ." Howard realizes he's losing it here. He licks his dry lips and can taste the sour drops of sweat. "Oh, fuck it. Am I under arrest? If I am, I want to talk to a lawyer."

This is the moment of decision for the deputy.

His training says his probable cause is dicey, but his instinct says he would regret letting this one go. Furthermore, he does not like that the suspect made the experienced move of forcing the issue of arrest while simultaneously invoking his right to a lawyer.

What the hell, he decides, *let the prosecutor sort out the legal crap.*

An ace, king, and a seven come out on the flop, a rainbow. Wyatt regrets for a moment mucking his ace-deuce off suit, even while knowing this is the right move, particularly in early position.

Wyatt folded not just because he did not like his hand, but because he is not mentally in the game. The other players are jawing as usual, mostly about crime and politics and office gossip, random riffs, but Wyatt's mind is skipping from Howard to Suki, who has been making it clear that children are part of her vision of the future. This ups the stakes.

Graham, just to the left of Wyatt, cannot remember if this is a one-dollar betting round or a two-dollar round, so he checks and sips his water. He is a sober alcoholic who played college football and has a master's degree in philosophy.

Jay, just out of a robbery trial, a stout poker aficionado who plays more than anyone else at the table, has queen-jack, and he bets out though he knows he should check.

"I'm here to gamble."

Liza, the supervisor from the identity theft unit, arguably the most grossly understaffed trial unit in a chronically understaffed office, calls with her pocket eights, too tired to think through all the good reasons to fold.

"Why am I doing this?" she asks, splashing the pot.

Mike has a pocket pair of kings and the one on the table gives him a set. He pauses, considering whether to raise or slow play. He raised before the flop and nobody reraised, so he rules out pocket aces as likely competition.

Their monthly game takes place at Mike's house in the dining room he converted to a poker room. The ceilings are coved and the walls are green and hanging behind Mike is a framed movie poster from *Pulp Fiction*. Uma Thurman lies on an unmade bed with a cigarette, a gun, and a paperback in the foreground. Small speakers in the corners carry music from a stereo in the main room and a compilation CD Mike made is playing, currently Tears for Fears' "Everybody Wants to Rule the World."

Mike sets two blue chips out in front of him, a raise. He forgoes the slow play opportunity because he is going to have plenty of callers and his raise will likely be misread anyway.

Mix it up.

"Fuck," Liza says, shaking her head, "I knew I should have folded."

Tears for Fears segues into a Sid Vicious cover of "My Way" on the CD and Josh, a prosecutor who just finished trying a murder case for the third time—it was reversed twice on technicalities— looks over in mock horror.

"Who in the hell is this?"

"Sid Vicious doing Frank Sinatra."

"Sounds like he's doing him in the ass."

Julian, a drug unit trial prosecutor, laughs and calls with his ace-eight suited. Though his eight is a weak kicker, hope springs eternal.

After thinking about it, Bennet says, "Raise, huh?"

"Put two blue chips in," Josh says.

"Relax, Rumpelstiltskin."

"Rumpelstiltskin?"

Bennet, a homicide detective Wyatt used to work with, is unflappable. He pays no mind to Josh, makes Mike for an ace, maybe ace-king, figuring he would slow play if he had a set, and decides to stick around for the action with his king-ten.

"Call," Bennet says, putting his two chips out.

"Fucking Jay," Josh mutters, angry that Jay bet into Mike when he should have expected the raise. He calls, bitterly.

Wyatt and Mike exchange a look, as they have the same thought: *Josh is likely on a gutshot draw.*

Adam, a former prosecutor turned politician, also catches Mike's look and has the same thought, though it does not affect his play. The flop missed him and so he folds.

"It's just a couple dollars," Jay says.

"Wouldn't be prudent."

Graham likes his hand, but calls instead of suffering the abuse that follows a check-raise.

"Fat pot," Jay says, also calling.

"What am I doing?" Liza repeats as she calls.

Adam burns a card, then lays out the turn card, a queen of diamonds.

"'Don't you draw the queen of diamonds, boy.'"

"'She'll beat you if she's able.'"

"'The queen of hearts is always your best bet.'"

For the approximately one millionth time, the Eagles are quoted at a poker game, and Mike decides he'll follow his compilation CD with *Hotel California,* the title song being one of his longtime favorite addiction tunes.

"Do you think I should marry Suki?" Wyatt asks Mike.

"Sure," Mike says, watching reactions to the queen.

"I'm serious, Counselor."

"You're forty. You should get married."

"You're almost forty. You're not married."

"But you've already got your money in the pot, so to speak, with Suki, and I'm not there yet with June."

"Almost everything in life," Adam says, "can be analogized to poker."

"Graham," Josh says, "the action's on you. Check?"

"I like marriage," Jay says.

"Jay, what the fuck world do you go back and forth from?" Josh asks.

Graham bets one dollar.

"Nice bet," Josh says. "Except it's one dollar on the flop and before the flop. Two dollars on the turn and river, as it's been for the last four years. I know it's complicated."

Graham shrugs and pushes out another blue chip. "I wish kids hadn't been so mean to you on the playground."

Jay nods in drunken agreement, "Yeah," and then calls.

"What am I doing to myself?" Liza asks, also calling.

Based on table observation, Mike believes the queen did not make anyone's hand, and so he thinks he still has the best hand. There are a lot of river cards that could potentially beat him, but he wants to make the draws pay, so he raises.

Force your opponents into difficult decisions.

Julian grimaces. He hates to fold aces, but he runs through a quick list of some of the better hands possibly out there: *ace with a better kicker, two pair, a set, a straight,* and he lets go.

Bennet calculates his pot odds. He figures he has about a one-in-twelve chance of drawing a jack on the river, which would give him a straight. Calling will cost him four dollars and there is about forty dollars in the pot, so he is getting ten-to-one on his money, but he would need better than twelve-to-one odds to justify a call and should, mathematically speaking, fold. *Except,* the pot is likely going to grow and improve his odds, and so he can justify calling.

"Call."

Josh, needing a ten for a straight, goes through the same math, and comes to the same conclusion, *long shot, but fat pot.*

"Call."

Graham considers reraising, but by now he sees the straight possibilities and just calls Mike's raise, as do Jay and Liza.

"Let's see the river."

Adam, with a dramatic flourish, burns a card and then slowly turns the river card up from the deck, looks at it himself, laughs, then lays the queen beside its sister for all to see.

"Siegfried and Roy on the board."

Graham bets a dollar, and then notices that he has a full house.

"Two dollars on this round," Mike reminds him.

"My bad."

"You better not fucking win this pot," Josh says to Graham. "You just better fucking not."

Jay has trip queens and though he recognizes it is probably a losing hand he calls because it *could* be a winning hand.

"Cards were just good enough to get me in trouble," Liza says, folding.

Graham laughs at this, which turns heads.

"You better fucking *not* win this pot," Josh repeats.

Graham's laughter worries Mike. Giddy players usually have good cards. Mike looks at Wyatt and again they can tell they have the same thought: *goddamn Graham.* Anytime they think poker, or life, is something that can be controlled or predicted, there's Graham.

"Raise," Mike says, unwilling to slow down, as Graham would have to hold pocket aces or pocket queens to beat him. Though this is possible, it is inconsistent with the betting, even taking into account Graham's randomness. He puts Graham on king-queen at best. "So," he says, turning to Wyatt, "are you going to marry her?"

"I should."

"You got that right at least."

Grateful for Mike's raise because it gives him an additional reason to fold, Bennet mucks his cards.

"Trouble waiting to happen," he says.

"Like life," Adam says.

Though the queen improved Josh's hand, he suspects it is just good enough that he cannot get away from it when he should. He weighs the possibility that Mike is now stuck with three pair to choose from, known as a Selby, and that Graham and Jay are completely out to lunch. He thinks the latter if a good bet, but the former *unfuckinglikely. Mike's not going to raise with a Selby, he's probably got pocket aces or kings.* He decides to hold on to the few chips he has left, regrets playing to see the turn card.

"I fucking hate poker," he says, folding, disgusted with himself, the game, and the world.

"Call," Graham says.

Mike is expressionlessly pleased. The pot is rich by their standards and it is his—if Graham had him beat he would have raised. Mike does not care about the money or the results of any given night because he believes poker is a single lifelong game with breaks and changing players and it is not over until you give it up permanently or you die, but nonetheless he wants this pot.

"You really think I should marry her," Wyatt says.

"Sure," Mike says, "what's life without risk?"

"You planning to call the raise?" Josh asks Jay.

"I don't know," Jay says, stalling to annoy Josh. "Right now I need a scotch, though."

"Yeah," Josh says, "that's just what you need."

Julian hands him the green bottle of Laphroaig, and Jay smiles as he half fills his lowball glass.

"Side bet," Wyatt proposes to Mike. "If you win the pot, I'll quit pestering you about signing up Marvin as a CI. If you lose, you sign up Marvin or the midget."

"The midget?"

"Yeah, I think he's got a little info."

"Just a *little?*" Josh says, grinning.

"How about if I win you marry Suki?" Mike says.

"How about if we finish this hand?" Liza says.

"Are you going to win?" Wyatt asks Mike.

"Probably."

Jay, mistaking candidness for weakness, and simply unable to fold this late in the game, calls.

Mike flips over the pocket kings, an apparent winner.

"Well played, Jay," Josh says as Jay mucks his cards.

Jay shrugs. "I'm an addict."

Eyes turn to Graham, who slow-rolls his pocket aces. Astonishment, groans, laughter, and facetious applause erupt around the table.

Be Zen, Mike reminds himself. *Put on the Eagles.*

"Did we have a side bet?" Wyatt says. "I think I just won. Gotta love this game."

"You didn't *raise* with that hand?" Josh says, staring at Graham, shaking his head.

Graham smiles as he spreads his hands out in a circle around the chips and drags them in, the large pile clacking and shifting, so many chips that some slip out of his grip. He tries not to laugh, but fails.

"Play Sid Vicious doing Sinatra again."

The barred door is electronically clanked open and Ted Haller enters the jail and walks alone down the empty hallway under flickering fluorescent lights. Ted has a slight post-lunch buzz going, just enough so that he is indifferent to the dank air and bad vibes.

One of the many advantages of being a prosecutor is that you do not have to visit clients in jail. Ted, a public defender for twenty-three years, feels he is serving a penance every time he enters what he calls the Gray Bar Hotel. He is known by other lawyers and some of his clients as "Cocktail Ted" because of his penchant for bourbon lunches that precede afternoon visits.

The guard at the next check stop knows Ted—the guards and the lawyers are all well acquainted in Pierce County—and opens Visitors' Room F for him. A few minutes later his client, Howard, is brought in and they are left alone in the small drab space with no windows and two wooden chairs. Between them is a green metal desk.

"Hello, Lars," Ted says, setting his manila folder on the desk. "I'm Ted Haller. I'm your lawyer."

I'm fucked, Howard thinks as he checks out this pudgy balding middle-aged man wearing worn khakis and an old tweed coat.

"Do you prefer Lars, or Howard? There seems to be some confusion about your name on the charging documents."

"My name is Howard. Friends call me Lars."

Ted recognizes all the symptoms of a tweeker: pasty skin, twitchy limbs, a hollow stare, and the scabs on his hands and forearms from meth bugs—imaginary creatures tweekers scratch incessantly. In Ted's experience it takes eight to twelve weeks of cold turkey before tweekers can communicate. Even then, though, a dialogue with a tweeker is roughly akin to one with a snotty ten-year-old.

Because of seniority, Ted is one of the attorneys at the Department of Assigned Counsel who assign cases, and he awarded himself this one because it was solid and he expected it would be a quick guilty plea. The strung-out defendant left him a voice-mail message implying that he just wanted to take a deal and get it over with.

Once, ten years ago, Ted defended a man he actually thought was innocent and this was so stressful, so outside his comfort zone, he swore he would never to it again. He is grateful the situation has not arisen since.

"I understand you just got back from Western State," Ted says, "and the docs declared you competent."

"Yeah, I'm not crazy, I was just squishing."

"Right, okay."

"Should I have pretended I was mental?"

"No, no, no sense in that, Lars. Sometimes it's good for the soul to just take responsibility. And it can reduce your prison term, too." Receiving no reaction, Ted continues. "Looks like they caught you cold with a very large amount of pseudoephedrine. No pun intended."

"What?"

"Caught you *cold* with pseudoephedrine."

Howard stares back, eyes blinking.

"Never mind," Ted continues. "You had six pounds of pseudo. That's a boatload, Lars. The prosecutor is likely going to take this case pretty seriously."

"It's just one case, they have thousands."

"You can't slip under the radar screen with a quantity like that."

"It wasn't mine."

Let the lying begin.

"You said in your message that you just wanted to get this over with," Ted continues, ignoring the customary mendacity. "Get the best deal you can?"

"I was out of my mind when I left that message."

Ted nods, though Howard did not sound any worse than any other tweeker in any other voice mail.

"I've been talking to some of the guys," Howard continues, "and I'm pretty confident I can beat this."

Shit, the jailhouse lawyers have gotten to him.

"So you've been taking advice from fellow inmates?"

"Some of the guys know a lot."

"If they know so fucking much," Ted says, shifting from his empathetic voice to his authoritative voice, "why are they in jail?"

Any defense lawyer has seen this cycle before: the defendant initially wants to unburden himself through confession, but then the consequences of confession begin to occur to him, and he decides that everyone else is getting away with murder, figuratively or literally, and so why shouldn't he?

Is it not his right as an American—nay, his obligation—to get a lawyer, to deny responsibility, to squeeze through the technical cracks, to beat the system?

"First thing we need to do is set up a bail hearing," Howard advises Ted.

"You're looking at fifty-one to sixty-eight months if you're convicted at trial, Lars." Ted mistakenly thinks Howard has no criminal history, because none comes up under his current moniker. "High end for sure if you go to trial."

"I can't do that much time."

"What if I could get a plea for something less?" Ted tries. "Maybe a DOSA. You're familiar with the DOSA program, right?"

"It cuts your prison time in, like, half?"

"That's the general idea. Let's say you receive a sixty-month DOSA. You only have to serve the first thirty months in prison, and you get half off for good behavior, so that cuts the thirty to fifteen, and the Department of Corrections will release you to a halfway house about six months before the fifteen months are up." Ted smiles, always eager to deliver the money line. "So you serve about *nine months* on a sixty-month sentence!"

"No bullshit?"

"No bullshit, Lars. In theory you're supposed to do drug treatment for a couple years after you're out, but it's not really enforced."

"What if you screw up the treatment?"

"Everybody does. Once you're out it's almost impossible to get thrown back in jail."

"DOSA?"

"Right. Drug Offender Sentencing Alternative."

"Sounds okay, but I think we can get the evidence suppressed."

"What?"

"I don't want to plea," he says, increasingly twitchy. "I want to get the evidence suppressed. Then the case gets dismissed."

"Yes, I know how it works."

"So we'll do a bail hearing, then a hearing to get the evidence suppressed?"

The only thing I'm suppressing is an urge to bitch-slap your head.

"The cop was out to get me," Howard continues. "It was a pretentious stop."

"A *what?*"

"A pretentious stop. Judge Sanders says you can't do that in Washington. Some of the guys in here are friends with him. He's on the Washington Supreme Court."

"Yes, I know who the fuck *Justice* Sanders is," Ted says, surprising Howard with the f-bomb, "and I'm sure everyone in gray pajamas claims to be his friend."

"Sanders made pretentious stops illegal."

"It's called a 'pretextual stop.' " *Idiot jailhouse lawyers.* "Not a *pretentious* stop."

"Oh."

Ted sighs in a long exhalation, not caring if his bourbon breath envelops his client. Sometimes Ted hates his job—most of the time, in fact.

"I can pursue the suppression motions if you want," Ted finally says, "but the prosecutor will withdraw the DOSA offer if I do."

"Can they do that?"

"Yes."

"Bastards."

"Actually, many of them are women."

"Are we winning the war on drugs?" Mike repeats the question back to the interviewer from MSNBC, a standard gambit to clarify and buy time to think. Working late, he had to cancel his date with June. Sometimes he wishes he could go back to grad school and just read piles of books.

"You're in the trenches," the reporter says. "Is victory in sight from your perspective?"

People want the truth?

A cousin of his, a politician, told him this once—people want the truth and will not hold it against you for telling them. He would like to believe this.

"War is not really a useful metaphor," he says, starting off with his stock answer. "Drug use has been with us forever, always will be."

"Why do you think that is?"

"People like to feel good."

"So you're saying we're never going to win this war?"

"Again, war is not a useful metaphor."

"So if war isn't a useful metaphor, what is?"

"Realism is useful."

"And by that you mean?"

He stares up past the Cobain poster at a small ball of water slowly forming on his ceiling, not yet heavy enough to drop.

"People like their drugs," he says. "People like caffeine, alcohol, nicotine, painkillers, antidepressants. People like to alter their consciousness."

"Okay, but what about methamphetamine? Can we eliminate meth use?"

Mike listens to reporters carefully to gauge their angle, Googles them when he can, but he did not have time with this one.

"Not until the next drug *du jour* comes around."

"So what do we do in the meantime?"

Kill all the meth cooks?

"Two-prong approach to stop the bleeding," he says. "Cut supply, and cut demand. Right now, however, we don't have sufficient resources to do either, so we need to be more innovative."

"How do you cut supply?"

"Shut down sales of ephedrine or pseudoephedrine for starters, but the pharmaceutical companies have been blocking that for years. Billions of dollars are at stake. The corporate profit margin on pseudoephedrine would embarrass most drug dealers."

"Isn't Congress considering a bill this session?"

"Yes, Senator Cantwell is working on it, it's called the Combat Meth Act, and it's been tacked onto the Patriot Act, but even if we could cut off the legal sources for pseudo, there's still the black market, which will expand to meet the demand."

"Okay, so how do you cut demand, then?"

"We need to work with the addicts, get innovative in that area as well."

"What drives people to damaging drugs?"

People want the truth.

"You got me."

"What?"

"I don't know why people want to screw up their lives chasing drugs or money or sex or their obsession of choice. I don't know why politicians destroy their careers and reputations over petty bribes or sex with an intern. I don't get compulsive behavior. Of course, I don't even know how to work a microwave."

"Good night," one of his attorneys says on her way out, waving her umbrella.

"I'm leaving, too," Cort announces, stepping out into the hallway in his blue raincoat. "The Xerox machine is broken again, by the way. I've alerted *the others*."

Taken from the television series, *Lost*, "the others" is Cort's reference to office administration.

"Good night."

"What?"

"Nothing, I was just saying good night to the attorneys."

"Oh, late night for you there."

"Yeah."

"So do you feel like your trial unit, right there on the front lines, can see any progress?"

"As much progress as possible when you have thirteen attorneys handling about twenty-five hundred cases a year. And most of the attorneys in the unit, including me, are also handling homicide cases. We have over seventy defendants in the jail with pending homicides. There are more murderers in our jail than there are felony attorneys in our office."

"You're swamped."

"We're drowning. And the meth tsunami is rolling east."

Sensing that the interview is detouring, the reporter regroups. "You said earlier that people will always want to alter their consciousness?"

"One way or another, not necessarily in a destructive way."

"So why do people choose methamphetamine?"

"It's cheap, fast, and easy to make. Meth is the lazy way to alter consciousness."

He can hear the reporter typing again.

"The problem," Mike continues, "one of the problems, is that we've cried wolf too many times—about pot and heroin, for example—and now people are understandably slow to accept that we really do have a drug that's like putting your brain in a frying pan."

"You know who Norm Stamper is?"

"Former Seattle police chief."

"He's been doing op-ed pieces advocating for the legalization of all drugs, including meth."

"I think it's a good dialogue to open up."

"So you think legalization is a good idea?"

"No, I think a *dialogue* is a good idea."

"Stamper argues that drug use and abuse would not increase with legalization."

"I don't think that's realistic."

"Stamper believes legalization will dramatically reduce the public expenses of incarceration and law enforcement, and that it will put violent drug dealers and home meth labs out of business. He argues for letting the government sell it and tax it and regulate it."

And there's the reporter's angle.

Though exhausted, Mike has managed to maneuver his way through this interview mostly on message—*need resources and innovation*—and he knows he should end this interview now.

"Do you think keeping drugs illegal is reducing the number of addicts or crime?" the reporter asks when Mike does not respond to the Stamper argument.

"Or wasted lives?"

"Right, is keeping drugs illegal, is the drug war . . . *working?*"

Bone-tired, Mike can no more answer this than he could tell

the reporter the meaning of life or whether God exists—though he believes there is a meaning to life and God does exist. He stares up at the drop of water, still clinging to the ceiling.

"You want my personal opinion on this? Not the position of the office, but my personal opinion?"

"Absolutely."

This, Mike knows, is the moment journalists seek—the breaking point where the interviewee tires of rhetoric and lets his guard down, puts himself at the mercy of the interviewer.

"I don't think you can do a comprehensive piece on drug abuse without discussing three other subjects: spirituality, consumerism, and stupidity."

"No?" *Tap, tap, tap,* the typing begins again.

"I'm going to have to quote P. J. O'Rourke here: 'No drug causes the fundamental ills of society. If we're looking for the source of our troubles, we shouldn't test people for drugs, we should test them for stupidity, ignorance, greed, and love of power.' "

"So where does what leave us?"

It leaves me wanting a drink.

"I think," Mike says, "that O'Rourke's point is that drugs are a symptom of bigger problems. And he should know, he's done a lot of drugs."

After pulling out of the conversation, Mike stares at the drop of water until it falls, disappearing into the rug. Then he rummages through a stack of correspondence and court orders overflowing from his in-box. He wonders if he should have blown off the interview and everything else and gone out with June, but right now he needs the satisfaction of checking things off his list, cleaning tasks off his desk.

On top is a letter he opens despite the prison return address:

DEAR SIR MR LAWSON,

IM CORRENTLY IN DEPARTMENT OF CORECTOINS. IM WANTING TO NOWE IF YOU WILL MAKE A DEAL FORE MY TEST TOMONY AGANST METH COOKS. I NOWE A LOT OF METH COOKS AND THEY DISTOYD MY LIFE AND MENY MORE. WHUT IM ASKIN IS A REDUTION IN MY SENTIC FOR MY TEST TOMONY. I DO NOWE THAT PRISON IS AND ISNOT THE ANSER FOR ME PLEAS CON CIDER THIS THANK YOU.

The aspiring informant signs above his inmate number with his real name, Garth Ericksen, and his proposed alias, "Rocky Sly," and Mike shakes his head, thinking what he often thinks in his job.

Nobody could make this crap up.

Beneath the tweeker letter is a scheduling order from Ted Haller setting motion dates and a bail hearing, which triggers Mike's curiosity because Cocktail Ted almost never notes up motions, almost never goes to trial.

Ted is famous for cajoling, coercing, and begging his clients to plead and thereby avoid the extra prison time that follows a trial. Celebrities may be acquitted, but for garden-variety defendants it is usually merely a question of "guilty" or "incredibly guilty."

The defendant's name on Ted's scheduling order is Lars Ulrich, a.k.a. Howard Schultz, and he is currently in custody.

Mike smiles as he picks up the phone, *the job does have many moments of joy.*

"If you had to arrest a mime," Suki asks Wyatt, "would you tell him he had a right to remain silent?"

"You're a nut, you know."

He is the nut, in her eyes, but she believes she can crack him, open him up and solve the puzzle inside as she likes to do.

They stroll the wide and wet pedestrian boulevard on the shore of the Foss Waterway, wearing dark sweaters and holding hands, a routine image on the new walkway. Seagulls hover and swoop above, occasionally perching on the metal rails separating the boats from the boulevard, eyes alert for food. A light breeze ruffles the water and rattles the halyards, which clank against sailboat masts with a hollow knocking. The red neon sign of Johnny's Dock, an old-school restaurant on the east side of the waterway, reflects off the rippled surface.

Just a few years ago there was nothing on the west side of this polluted waterway into Commencement Bay but dirt, garbage, puddles of toxic mud, and the occasional drug addict skulking in the dark. Now graceful boats rest in a well-maintained marina on the right of the walkway and modern condominiums rise on the left just south of the Tacoma Museum of Glass, all gleaming in the city lights. The sounds of socializing buzz out of the Blue Olive, a cocktail bar on the bottom floor of the condos.

This metamorphosis, known as the Thea Foss Revitalization Project, won the Outstanding Civil Engineering Achievement Award from the American Society of Civil Engineers in 2005, and is part of the basis of Wyatt's faith in Tacoma's future. He loves the city. Tacoma, he believes, is on the verge, a frontier town preparing for the boom that brings civilization and a sense of pride, held back only by the stubborn idiocy of lawlessness.

Sometimes Wyatt thinks he wants to be a golf course groundskeeper when he retires, maybe work at Ladenburg's links, something like Bill Murray in *Caddyshack,* a job where he would just come out at night to mow the lawn and practice putting and not deal with criminal miscreants.

"So what do you think?" Suki asks as they pass under a bright new street lamp.

"About what?"

"What we were talking about."

"About arresting a mime?"

"Before that."

"What were we talking about before that?"

Suki sighs. "Are you serious?"

Wyatt tries to quickly recall what they were talking about, but his mind has left the subject too far behind. "Yes, I guess I am."

"Why do you seem so ambivalent lately?"

"Oh, right. Well . . . I don't know. Do I seem ambivalent?"

"You even seem ambivalent about your ambivalence."

"What?"

"I'm serious. It started after I moved in, after we started seeing each other all the time, after you started seeing me lying around in sweats."

"Okay."

"Okay?" Suki stops, releases his hand. "That's what you have to say?"

"You're probably right. You are right. But it has nothing to do with your sweatpants."

"What does it have to do with?"

"I don't know." Wyatt shrugs.

"You're infuriating." Suki shakes her head. "Why are you ambivalent about this? You don't seem ambivalent about anything else in your life. You're not an ambivalent person, and yet . . . here we are."

They stand there facing each other in the outer circle of a lamp's glow, able to hear the electricity humming from the pole, and he cannot help but notice that she looks especially pretty in this light.

"I've just been distracted sometimes."

"Not sometimes, pretty constantly."

"Yeah?"

"Yeah."

"Sometimes cases consume me," he says, knowing it sounds lame. "It's just that . . ." He doesn't know where to take this.

"You really think it's this one case?" When he does not answer immediately, she replies for him. "It's not. I don't believe this is all about . . . this Howard guy, or whatever he represents to you."

"Well, I'm not seeing anyone else."

"I didn't say you were. Where did *that* come from?"

"What are you implying, then?"

"Just what I said. It seems like whatever is going on is about more than one case." Suki wipes the hair out of her face as the wind picks up, carrying dark rain clouds from the east. An Air Force cargo plane rumbles overhead on the heavily used flight path over downtown. "Have you scheduled our vacation yet?"

Wyatt grimaces. "Shit, sorry."

"Wyatt . . ."

"I just . . . forgot. Sorry."

"You just forgot?"

"Yes, sorry."

"Wyatt . . . have you checked out of this relationship?"

"No. I don't want to check out."

"So you're checking out without even *choosing* to?"

"I didn't say I was checked out."

"You didn't say you weren't."

"Okay, stop. You're worse than a lawyer."

"I'm just trying to figure out what's going on, to understand."

"I get that."

"So I can make good choices."

After a few seconds of silence, with the quietness bringing a sense of possible reconciliation and shared desire, Wyatt's cell phone rings.

Their eyes meet; Suki purses her lips. Wyatt hesitates, starts to speak, but then reaches for his phone.

"Christ almighty," Suki says.

"It's Mike," Wyatt explains, "calling from the office. It's probably business."

Howard wakes up to the sound of robins outside the window. Normally he would go back to sleep, but the adrenaline kicks in when he realizes he is out of the stifling Pierce County Jail. This, at least, is good.

As he lies in bed beside Brandy, who is snoring like a truck driver, disgusting him, he formulates a plan for the day. His options are limited because of the clunky ankle bracelet he wears from the Electronic Home Monitoring agency.

Ted Haller, giving in to Howard, set up a bail hearing and argued halfheartedly that Howard should be released on home monitoring until trial. The judge agreed over the prosecutor's objection. Howard attributed this to fine lawyering by Cocktail Ted, but the judge was only thinking about the county budget.

Because of jail overcrowding and the accompanying lawsuits, criminals in Pierce County are regularly set free before their sentences are completed, and so the judge accepted the opportunity to make a jail bed available. Howard pays ten dollars a day to the EHM agency and he is not costing the county bed space or meals. However, the cost of Howard's continuing criminal activity did not figure into the judge's calculations.

In the kitchen Howard finds Brandy and convinces her that he has no meth, so she might as well go to work and he will see the kids off to school.

"What are you going to do all day?" Brandy asks as he is ushering her out.

"I have to talk to my lawyer."

He likes saying *my lawyer.*

"All day?"

"Legal motions are complicated, you know. We've got a whole pretentious stop issue, like I already told you."

Three years ago when Howard was on EHM after assaulting his girlfriend, he moved back in with her and would not allow her to leave the house until his sentence was completed because, as he told her, it was all her fault. However, Brandy cannot be blamed for his arrest, so he allows her to leave the house and, furthermore, he needs her out.

"Make sure that Porsche and Joe are on their way in time," she says as he opens the front door.

"I think they're up." He saw Porsche walk into the bathroom in a long white T-shirt and, it seemed to him, nothing else. "At least Porsche is."

"Make sure they have some orange juice or something for breakfast."

"Hey, they got to school fine before I moved in here."

"No, they didn't get to school fine. They're both late and absent all the time. Especially when I work mornings. That's the reason I don't work much."

"You sure it's not just because you're lazy?"

"You're one to talk."

"I may be many shitty things, but I'm not lazy." He tugs up his pants, scratches his crotch. "I'm the freakin' king."

"Well, then prove it. Get cooking."

"Keep nagging me," he says, "and see where that gets you, bitch."

"I'm sorry, honey," she says, staying in the doorway, switching into a little-girl voice. "I just want to get highhhhhhh."

They kiss and wish each other a good day, imitating a normal couple, and Howard closes the door behind her with relief and excitement.

Half an hour later he has Joe out the door, dressed in his quasi-gang attire, limping only slightly on his sprained ankle.

Porsche stays back. She is half dressed for school in "winter pink" lipstick, eyeliner, her black choker, tight hip-hugging jeans, and, to his disappointment, a bra under a black and red band T-shirt emblazoned with stencils of the three members of the Yeah Yeah Yeahs. Her dirty blond hair is up in a ponytail.

"Mom will be pissed if she knows," Porsche says.

"'Cause she's usually so good about caring if you go to school?"

"She cares. She's just . . . you know, a tweeker. That's why this house is, like, a disgusting double-wide trailer or something."

Howard nods, glancing around the living room. The brown and orange shag rug looks like it hasn't been vacuumed since the 1970s, the black vinyl couch has a dirty plate on a crooked cushion, the coffee table has two empty Olde English "800" cans and a half-full glass of what appears to be orange juice and an overflowing ashtray, the beige walls are stained in patches, and there is cat hair everywhere even though Howard has never seen a cat. Some tweekers will vacuum endlessly, but apparently not Brandy.

Howard opens the mini blinds over the front window, just a slit in the middle. He hunches over, peeks out, closes them back up.

That's why they're called tweeker blinds, Porsche says to herself.

"Okay," he says, rubbing his hands together. "Let's break out the good shit." He shamelessly leers at Porsche. "Sound good? Yeah?"

She shrugs. "What do you have?"

"What do you think I have?"

"Mom said you didn't have any meth."

"Since when do you listen to your mom?"

Though Porsche refuses to beg, she flashes just enough enthusiasm to show a smile.

Howard hustles off into the bedroom and a few moments later he comes back out with a purple Crown Royal bag. He sits on the couch and out of the bag pulls an amber glass vial with crystals, a baggie with white powder, and a glass pipe. The baggie is stamped with a Superman logo.

Porsche sits beside him, crossing her legs, intently watching his actions.

"This is from one of my personal cooks," he says, holding up the baggie. "You can tell by the logo." He sets down the baggie on the coffee table, holds up the vial. "And this is ice, from the same cook."

"Yeah?"

"Home-cooked means better than ninety percent purity. The shit you kids get at school is probably thirty percent pure, at best."

Porsche nods, though numbers generally bore her.

"I picked up this shit when we were at the storage unit and hid it from your mom." He sets down the vial next to the baggie and pulls a razor blade, butane lighter, short wire rod, and mirror out of the purple bag. "It ain't easy hiding shit from your mom."

She nods knowingly and watches Howard shake the powder into a corner of the baggie and then tear off that piece of the baggie and pour the powder onto the mirror.

"Since you helped out that day," he says, chopping the lines up with practiced strokes, "I might not charge you for the drugs here."

"*Charge me?* Girls don't *pay* for drugs."

"Oh, yeah, they do."

"Well, *I* don't."

"You've never paid for drugs?"

"I have, but with, like, other girls. The guys always pay if we're partying with them. Everybody knows *that*."

"You have a boyfriend?" he asks, looking up from his chopping.

"No."

"Why not? You prefer girls?"

"Nooooo. Why do guys always say that, like they hope it's true?"

"It's sexy."

"*What's* sexy?"

"A pretty young girl with another pretty young girl."

"If the girls are into girls, how is it sexy for a guy?"

"It just is, hon, it just is."

"Guys are weird."

"Here's everything you need to know about guys." Howard enjoys sharing his wisdom. "Guys do everything for sex. All guys, from Bill Clinton to George Bush to everybody."

"*George Bush?* Does everything for sex?" She holds up her thumbs and forefingers in the W, not knowing this is the president's middle initial. "What*ever*."

"Why do you think he did cocaine? Just 'cause he liked to get high? No. Because girls are into guys with cocaine." He returns to chopping the lines, straightening them and lengthening them. "And you gotta figure George Bush had good coke. Like, straight from a Colombian drug lord."

Porsche, tuning in to the sexual drift, shrugs.

"You prefer snorting or smoking?" he asks.

Porsche shrugs again. "Whatever."

"Well, we're gonna do both. Best of both worlds."

Porsche has never smoked meth, thinking that smoking it was somehow stepping past a line she should not cross. When she snorted, she did not feel much, and decided the chunky tan powder was hardly meth at all, but the sort of bogus dope that dealers sold to those who did not know better. The high school junior who provided it to her dropped considerably in her estimation.

"The rush of smoking, plus the longer and smoother high of snorting," Howard continues, picking up the vial and tapping a couple of crystals into the pipe through a hole in the top of the bowl.

Howard has numerous theories about meth and its production and consumption, as people fully involved in an occupation or hobby do. He thinks he should start a meth blog with MySpace because there is so much erroneous tweeker lore.

He wants to title the blog, "Don't Meth with Me!"

Delicately holding the glass pipe to his lips, he flicks the lighter on, directs the flame under the bowl until the crystal starts to boil, and then quickly sucks in the white vapors with a raspy desperate breath.

Porsche watches, fascinated with the process.

His eyes close as he sucks out the last ember of light in the bowl, and he holds the hit for several seconds and then finally exhales, his whole body slumping forward in surrender as he does.

After a few seconds of silence, which Porsche senses she should not break the sanctity of, Howard sets down the pipe, picks up the wire rod, and cleans out the residue with the fastidiousness of an artist tending to his tools.

As the meth enters his bloodstream through his lungs and then pumps into his brain, his synapses start to fire and burn—*snap, crackle, and pop*—as the meth kicks on the dopamine neurotransmitters and he starts to feel like Superman again.

I, I, I am Superman and I can do anything. . . .

He loads a jagged crystal of ice into the pipe and hands it to Porsche, who receives it carefully with both hands. She notes that her crystal is smaller than the one he smoked and she wonders if he is looking out for her or just being stingy.

"Put it in your mouth."

Closing her lips lightly around the end of the glass, Porsche watches as Howard moves the lighter flame under the bowl and the crystal starts to melt.

"Suck."

Ignoring what sounds like a sexual edge to the word, she breathes in the vapors. At first she does not feel anything and so she looks at Howard.

"Hold it in."

Her eyes grow big and wide as she does, and then she opens her mouth in an O and the smoke comes out in a thin stream.

"Good girl."

And then she feels it—a tingle and her heart thumping and she feels the rush sweep her to the edge of euphoria, but not quite there.

"It's hitting you," Howard says, smiling, watching.

"Uh-huh."

"That's just a taste."

She has smoked pot, dropped X, and drunk plenty of alcohol, but the high coming on is different—it fills her with confidence instead of insecurity, something no drug has done for her before.

"Should I have . . . more," she asks.

Porsche wonders if she made a mistake by letting him know what she was thinking, wonders if he can tell just how badly she wants more.

"We're going to play a little game," Howard says.

"Yeah?"

"It's called 'strip and snort.' "

"Strip and snort?"

"Yep. Smoking is a nice instant rush, but snorting prolongs it all goddamn day."

"So you're geeking."

"What?"

"That's what it's called at school—you're geeking if you're stoned."

"Well, you're going to like geeking." Howard starts chopping out the meth on the mirror. "For each item of clothes you remove you get one snort."

Porsche stares at him for a beat, trying to gauge if he is serious. She quickly realizes he is, and that she is possibly in over her head, but she has dealt with older guys before and feels she can hold her own.

"That's sort of juvenile," she says. "Don't you think?"

"I think . . . you just missed your turn."

Howard holds up his leg with the ankle bracelet and makes a show of taking off his sock, which grosses Porsche out. After he removes his other sock, he leans over and puts a snort straw to a short line and quickly huffs it all. Sitting up, sniffling, he smiles at Porsche.

She removes her socks, revealing pink-painted toenails.

"Nice," he says, "but keep going."

"Keep going?"

"Yeah, you skipped your first turn, so you're one behind. Keep going."

"That's . . . dumb."

"You want to play or not?"

"Not."

Howard shrugs. "More for me."

He begins cutting another line out from the pile in the corner of the mirror. Porsche, heart pattering, sees her reflection there, her flushed face, distorted but pretty, *desirable,* as the white line takes shape.

"Okay," she says, "whatever," and she unceremoniously removes her T-shirt. Her bra is white and plain.

"Small tits," Howard comments.

"So? Models have small boobs."

"Only homos like models."

"The singer of the White Stripes married a model."

"Homo."

"And Eddie Vedder dates Jill McCormick, a model."

"Homo."

"No, he's not."

"Yes, he is."

Porsche, surprised by Howard's insistence, decides to drop this course of conversation, though she feels bad about not carrying on a defense of Eddie Vedder, her choice for cutest older man in the world.

Howard bends down and fine-tunes the line on the mirror, which she assumes, hopes, is hers. He hands her the straw. Imitating what she observed, she puts the straw in one nostril, gently closes the other nostril with her index finger, leans down, and clumsily guides the straw toward the line and when it is there she breathes in deeply and slides the straw over the line, the white powder disappearing, *poof.*

"You don't have to hold your breath."

She exhales as she sits back up and the only thing that hits her right away is the burning in her nose, but she knew there would be some of that and accepts the pain.

"That was just a toddler line," Howard says.

Gulping, Porsche feels the meth drip from her nasal passages into her throat, a dry and tinny taste.

"Nice tat," she says, looking at his forearm as he chops up another line.

"Yeah, one of these days we'll get you one."

"Seriously?" It sounds cool at the moment. "Like what?"

"Something with . . . blood and roses."

"Mom will freak out."

Shifting nostrils, Howard whiffs up a line and turns to Porsche with a maniacal heaven-is-just-around-the-corner grin. "Want to feed the other half of your brain?" he asks, as if inhaling a drug through just one nostril would leave a user only half affected.

Porsche nods, knowing what he will say next.

"Lose the jeans, then."

Shrugging, as indifferently as she can manage, she stands and wiggles down the jeans. She is wearing plain white full-back bikini underwear.

"Step out of the jeans and turn in a circle."

Unsure why, she does so, goose pimples rising.

Howard leans back and unabashedly stares. "Skinny," he says, "but nice ass anyway."

She makes a face over her shoulder and quickly sits back down. A few girls at her school are on what they call the "Jenny Crank" diet, but she is naturally slender.

Howard chops up another small line and hands Porsche the straw. He stares at her ass as she leans over to fill the left nostril and she does not flinch as he slaps the top of her cheeks over the worn cotton.

"You got the hang of it now," he says.

She whips her head back and wipes her nose. "This is so much better than boys have at school," she says, suddenly in an open and generous mood.

Howard smiles, calculating that so far he has only given her about twenty dollars' worth of meth, *a bargain*. He appraises her gangly body, touches a hip bone jutting out over the elastic of the bikini panties.

"Are you the prettiest girl at your school?"

"No," she says, moving his hand away.

"I have to admit something."

"Yeah?"

"You *do* have the body of a model."

"You said only homos like models."

"I mean famous models. You've got the body, without being a famous stuck-up bitch. When you're older, boys are going to be falling all over each other to get to you."

"Thanks." Breathing rapidly, unconsciously grinding her jaw and rolling her tight shoulders, Porsche looks around the room. She can hear the rain pattering on the roof, weirdly loud. "We should clean this fucking ugly-ass house up."

Howard laughs.

"I'm serious. I hate what a fucking pigsty this house is." She stands up in her underwear, making no motion for her clothes. "Let's clean it up."

"That black choker doesn't match your white undies."

"Black and white always match." She tilts her head, puts her hands on her hips. "Are you gonna help?"

Sex is more where Howard would like Porsche's peppiness channeled, but they have plenty of days and nights of Electronic Home Monitoring ahead, and he knows he will have her soon and often, *welcome to my world, princess.*

"If you're good," he says, "I'll give you a 'lude later."

"What?"

"A Quaalude, to come down."

"You have those, too?"

"Just for my very favorite girls."

At 4:20 p.m. Ted's legal assistant faxes Mike the Howard Schultz brief for the suppression motion, which is set the next morning at nine-thirty. Ted left his office after lunch to go play golf, taking advantage of a rare fall day without rain. He told his assistant to fax the brief before she left for the day, *no rush, it's already late.*

The brief was due two weeks ago. However, for most criminal defense attorneys it is customary to deliver their briefs shortly before the motion. Then the prosecutor must either continue the motion, thereby delaying the case, or go forward less than fully prepared. Prosecutors often opt for the latter because continuances invariably work to the advantage of the defense—witnesses disappear, memories fade, other cases take priority. Furthermore, prosecutors often find it is easier to respond orally in court than spend hours they do not have writing a brief.

Sometimes defense attorneys push the prosecutor into this decision by design, sometimes it just works out that way. Though Ted is familiar with the popular obstructionist theory of criminal defense—stall and obfuscate—he will not go out of his way to do either. One thing he has in common with local prosecutors is too many cases and not enough of a life.

Nearly six hours after Ted left his office, Mike is checking his e-mail and in-box, about to call it a day. He finds the fax from Ted and this halts his exit. He spends a few minutes skimming the brief, making notes in the margins. Then he goes online and makes copies of the two cases Ted cites, though he is already familiar with both.

Shockingly to Mike, Ted has spotted the issue. Though the

leading case Ted relies on is absurd, a close five-to-four decision, it is still good law and it appears on its face to apply to the
facts.

Because there is not time to type up a brief, Mike hand-writes
a memo that he will use as a crib sheet for oral argument. By midnight he goes home, hoping for five hours of sleep, about an hour
less than his weekday standard.

His bed is king-sized, and the walls are light blue, *teal,* because
Mary, the team chief of the Special Assault Unit, a fellow night
owl, told him that teal was a soothing color and would help him
sleep. Especially, she added, if he used Ambien. A few people in his
office are on drugs, antidepressants, but Mike has never been
truly depressed and he will not use chemical remedies for sleep,
except for alcohol.

A variety of matters can keep him awake, mostly related to a
constant sense of falling behind in his workload, but this has been
happening less since he resumed meditating. When he was a trial
attorney in the Special Assault Unit, SAU, his bouts of sleepless-
ness were sometimes adrenaline-charged and he did not mind
losing sleep when he was in trial. In this he recognizes that trial
lawyers are like drug addicts, *living for the high.*

Tonight a touch of the adrenaline is back. He is looking forward to court tomorrow and his mind is playing through arguments: what Ted will open with, what he will respond, what Ted
will counter, what the judge will likely ask, and on and on. He
canceled another date with June because he knew he would be
bad company.

Before his alarm goes off he wakes up, instantly alert, which
only happens on trial days. Though a motion is to a trial as a skit
is to a play, a miniature of a drama, he is glad to have some of that
same showtime buzz. He pads into the kitchen in his boxers and

drinks a glass of orange juice mixed with cranberry and munches down a handful of granola from a box of cereal.

Patti Smith's *Wave* is already loaded in the stereo and he turns it on and clicks to track three, an ever-reliable picker-upper. Speakers throughout the house blast out the screeching guitar and then the pounding drums and then the bass line and chords and finally her awesome heroin voice, *"So you wanna be a rock and roll star, then listen now to what I say . . ."*

Showering, shaving, and brushing his teeth takes about fifteen minutes. He plays through all the likely arguments again in his head, making sure he has not missed one, knowing there is always one. Trials are a game that move as you play.

Picking a suit for court is easy, as he owns nothing but blue standards from Brooks Brothers, and the choice of shirt is equally uncomplicated, as he has only white button-down oxfords. Most of his dates have been disconcerted by his monochromatic wardrobe, except for June, who seems strangely pleased.

Just before he exits the house, Mike picks out a watch, a traditional white-dial Timex with black hands and leather strap. Though he consciously minimizes his possessions, he has an uncharacteristic indulgence in his nightstand drawer: twelve watches, four Timex, three L. L. Bean, three Orvis, one Swiss Army, and one Rat Pack–style Rolex from the early sixties.

Sometimes late at night, when it is especially quiet, he can hear ticking from the drawer.

LUCK OF THE DRAW

At nine in the morning the presiding court comes to order with the proverbial rap of the gavel. This triggers a Pavlovian response in the lawyers, their heads turning toward the judge's empty chair, which is flanked by the flags of Washington and the United States.

Here the attorneys and defendants gather before being sent out to trial, and it is heated up with bodies that exceed the fire code limits. Four dozen lawyers stand in shifting groups around the counsel tables and about a dozen more sit in the jury box. Behind them, about fifty people line the bench seats of the gallery, mostly out-of-custody defendants, but also their friends, lovers, and relatives, some of whom are victims or witnesses in their cases. Court can be a family affair.

The in-custody defendants sit in the adjoining jury room, enjoying comfortable seats that are second only to those of the judges. When his or her case is up each defendant is escorted out by two of the six guards standing by.

After the judicial assistant calls the court to order, Judge Sorensen enters, gray-haired and black-robed. He takes the bench with the beleaguered countenance of a twice-bitten lion-tamer working for a low-budget circus.

When the Howard Schultz case is called Mike responds, "Present and ready, Your Honor."

Most drug trials are resolved at the motions stage—if the defense fails to suppress the evidence the next logical step is a plea.

"Thank you, Mr. Lawson. Mr. Haller?"

"What?" Ted says, looking up from a conversation with a young female prosecutor he has a crush on.

"You want to be assigned out for a motion?"

"Sure."

"Is your client present?"

"I don't know." Ted looks in the gallery. "Mr. Ulrich? Or Mr. Schultz?"

Howard raises his hand from the back row. He is sitting with Porsche, who is wearing a lavender camisole top, and the sight of a defendant sitting with a twelve-year-old girl confirms Judge Sorensen's usual despair and he checks the file to make sure it is not a child-molest case. Though the judge cannot tell from his perch fifty feet away, both Howard and Porsche are shaking from their morning bump.

"My client is here," Ted reports.

"Yes, I see."

"But if there aren't any courtrooms available . . ." Ted shrugs. Though he does not complete the sentence, the meaning is clear: there usually are not enough courtrooms to go around, so some of the cases need to be continued and Ted is happy to be one of those continuances.

"How long will the motion take?" the judge asks.

"About an hour," Mike says.

"Or two," Ted says.

"Judge Stuber is available."

Eccentric is the word most often applied to Judge Eva Stuber. She has two dozen cats, writes romance novels under a nom de plume, and is given to wearing colorful hats and making impolitic statements.

As Mike steps out into the hallway with the manila court file, Wyatt joins him.

"I couldn't breathe in there," Wyatt says.

"I think it's the oxygen deprivation that makes everyone in there act half crazy."

"Did you see him?"

"Ted will bring him to Stuber's court."

"She's the cat lady, right?"

"The very one."

They step down the hallway, their footsteps echoing on the granite as they pass the usual cast of characters: suited lawyers, uniformed police officers waiting idly to testify, plainclothes detectives using cell phones, unkempt defendants and their girlfriends, and numerous children with no apparent supervision.

"Have you seen the deputy this morning?" Mike asks.

"Yeah, he went up to the café on eleven. I told him we would call when we were assigned out." Wyatt pulls out his cell phone and pages him, punching in the courtroom number. "The kid looks like Howdy Doody, by the way."

When they enter the courtroom they are warmly greeted by the judicial assistant and the court reporter, everyone taking a moment for personal and professional updates. One of the pleasures of working in the courthouse are the mostly good-humored people who maintain an upbeat attitude despite the wretchedness they see every day.

Judicial assistants and court reporters have seen up close the damage defendants wreak, they've heard from the victims, and they develop the same style of gallows humor and protective cynicism as the lawyers. They tend to silently side with prosecutors because they appreciate veracity, accountability, and availability. The prosecutors are housed in the same asylum.

Wyatt sits in the gallery behind Mike, waiting to see Howard. After a few long minutes the tall doors of the court open. Porsche enters, and Howard steps in behind her, cocky in his cowboy boots.

Wyatt stares, *shorter than I expected.*

Other than that, Howard fits the descriptions Wyatt has been given: wiry, pale, long blond hair, goatee. He is wearing a long-sleeved sweatshirt with GOD CAN CHANGE HOPELESS DOPE FIENDS INTO DOPELESS HOPE FIENDS in block letters across the front, apparently trying to represent himself as rehabilitated and converted. Tweekers often have slogans on their clothes and Wyatt suspects it is because nobody listens to them.

Howard crosses over toward Ted, but on the way he feels Wyatt's gaze and meets it and it instantly unnerves him. Still, he stares back for a moment before looking away. He has heard on the street that Detective Wyatt James has been hunting for him and now he knows his face.

When Judge Stuber emerges from her chambers, her judicial assistant raps the gavel and everyone rises. Porsche stays in the first row of the gallery directly behind Wyatt.

"Good morning," the judge says, ready for the day's entertainment.

Mike stays on his feet while he calls the case for the record. "This is State versus Howard Schultz. The defendant is present out of custody, represented by counsel Ted Haller, who is also present. We're here on a 3.6 defense motion."

"You ready, Mr. Haller?"

Ted, wearing rumpled corduroy pants and a frayed blue blazer, is listening to Howard whisper when he suddenly hears the judge.

"What?" Ted says.

"Are you ready to proceed, Mr. Haller?"

"Yes, sure. Let's go."

"I had just clocked out."

"When you're off duty, do you respond if you witness a crime or an infraction?"

"Yes. I have."

"How many times have you pulled people over when you were off duty?"

"At least two. Once I saw what I thought was a drunk driver ahead of me and so I pulled him over."

"What caused you to pull the defendant's car over in this case?"

"Two things. The broken headlamp, and the fact that I recognized the Firebird from a previous stop."

"When was this previous stop?"

"A couple of weeks before this stop."

"At what point did you realize that the car with the broken driver's headlight was the Firebird you had contacted previously?"

"Not until it drove by me."

"Had you already decided to pull the car over?"

"I was already thinking about it, yes."

"Can you describe your previous contact with this Firebird?"

The deputy looks up at the judge, suddenly conversational. "I stopped the car once before for a broken taillamp. And it turned out the occupants had been buying boxes of pseudoephedrine at different stores, which is common for methamphetamine cooks and their runners."

Ted could object, but does not.

"Was the defendant Howard Schultz the driver during that first contact?" Mike asks.

"No," the deputy says, turning back to Mike. "He was a passenger."

"Was he arrested?"

Judges are generally control freaks, and Ted's lack of focu deference makes some spitting mad, but Judge Stuber likes T

"Call your first witness, Mr. Lawson."

Deputy Newton stands stiff and straight as the judge s him in, and he practically yells back, "Yes, Your Honor," befo ting down in the wooden chair.

Clean-shaven, hands fixed in lap, the young deputy has testified before and he is nervous on the stand even as Mike him through the easy preliminaries. When they progress stop, Mike pauses to let the deputy know it is game time. here on Mike works off a script.

"What was the first thing you noticed about the defe vehicle when you saw it driving toward you?"

"One of the headlamps was out."

"And what time was this?"

"About ten o'clock."

"At night?"

"Yes. Right."

"Are there any streetlights on that road?"

"Only at intersections."

"Were there intersections where you first saw the defe

"No."

"So the road was dark?"

"Yes."

"Was it raining?"

"Yes."

"Which headlight was out?"

"The driver's side."

"Did you consider that dangerous?"

"Yes."

"You weren't on duty at the time?"

"No, just the driver was."

"As the Firebird drove by you, could you tell who was driving?"

"No. I just recognized the car."

"What about the car was distinctive?"

"The hood had a half-finished fire-breathing bird painted on it. The rest was gray primer paint."

Mike and Judge Stuber exchange an amused glance, and Mike flips to another page of his script.

"What did you do after the defendant's car passed?"

"I performed a U-turn and followed him."

"Did you activate your wig-wag lights and siren?"

"Yes."

"And what did you intend to pull him over for?"

"The broken headlamp."

"Was the fact that you had a previous contact with him part of the reason you decided to pull him over?"

"Yes."

"Was the previous contact the *only* reason that you decided to pull the defendant over?"

"No."

"Was the previous contact the *main* reason that you decided to pull him over?"

"No."

"There was also the broken headlamp and the danger that potentially posed on the road?"

"Correct."

Mike's questions have become leading, but Ted barely objects during trials, let alone during a motions hearing. He considers objections to be in bad form and mostly ineffective.

"What did the defendant do when you activated your lights and sirens?"

"He sped up."

"What speed were you initially following him at?"

"About forty miles per hour, the legal limit."

"And what did he speed up to?"

"About fifty, maybe a little faster."

"What did you do?"

"Speed up to about sixty."

"And what did he do?"

"Sped up some more, swerved back and forth over the center line."

"And what did you do?"

"I sped up to about eighty."

"For how long did you pursue him?"

"I'm not sure, less than a minute. I started gaining on him, so he pulled over."

"What did you do then?"

"I contacted him at the driver's-side window."

"Did you tell him why you pulled him over?"

"Yes."

"What did you tell him?"

"That one of his headlamps was out and it was dangerous."

This establishes the gist of the record as to the stop, which was the entire focus of Ted's brief. Mike also details the steps of the eventual arrest. He believes the truth nearly always emerges in a courtroom, though sometimes it needs nudging.

After finishing up with a quick description of the bag's contents, which were discovered in the search incident to arrest, he thanks the deputy and sits down.

"Mr. Haller," the judge cues Ted, who is wiping off breakfast cereal stuck on his tie.

Howard, hunched over beside Ted, is scribbling notes at a mad pace. This is a defense attorney strategem to shut up their clients: hand them yellow pads and a pen and tell them to write down their thoughts.

"Yes," Ted says, rising, "okay, thank you."

Howard looks up from his pad and stares at Ted with something between an encouraging smile and a worried glare. Mike can tell that Howard is one of those defendants who would like to do the cross-examination himself, but is smart enough to know he needs a lawyer.

"Now, Deputy," Ted says, ignoring Howard and approaching the witness, "you, uh, recognized the car as it approached you?"

"Yes."

"I just want to be sure I get this right." Ted checks his legal pad. "You recognized the car because of the fire-breathing dragon thing on the hood?"

"Right."

"And you had recently stopped this same car?"

"Yes."

"And you arrested the driver for . . . what, manufacture of meth? After the first stop?"

"Possession of pseudoephedrine with intent to manufacture."

"Right, okay, thanks." Ted scratches his head, reminding Mike of the bumbling yet effective television detective Columbo. "And oftentimes when defendants are arrested they're released on bail, right?"

"Right."

"And in the meth world, the first thing tweekers usually do when they are out on bail is manufacture more meth to help them pay back bail money or hire a lawyer, right?"

Ted smiles up at the deputy, who is shocked to hear something this honest in a courtroom, *and from a criminal defense attorney, to boot.*

"Well, yeah, that's generally true," the deputy admits, hoping it is not a trick question.

"So as soon as you saw the Firebird with the fire-breathing dragon on the hood, you suspected possible criminal activity?"

"Yes, I did."

"You suspected criminal activity because the previous time you stopped this car, there *was* criminal activity."

"Right, yes."

"And that's good police work, to make connections like that, right?"

"I think so, yes."

"And you also noticed that there was a headlight out on the car, right?"

"Yes."

"And you were off duty at the time. You testified to that earlier?"

"Yes."

"And you were on your way home to . . . what?"

"To what?"

"I can see by the ring you're married, right?"

"Right."

"So you were headed home to see your wife."

"Oh, yes. Right."

"You have kids?"

"One girl. She's three."

"That's nice," Ted says, completely sincere. "What's her name?"

"Kendall."

"Nice name. Anyway, so you're on your way home to see your wife and Kendall."

"Right."

"It was almost eight, so you were probably late for dinner?"

"I don't remember, but probably."

"Have you ever pulled anyone over before when you were off duty and heading home?"

"Yes. As I testified earlier."

"Right. Twice before, you said."

"Twice that I can remember."

"And you've been a deputy for how long?"

"Almost a year."

"And in a year as a deputy, you can only think of two other times you've pulled someone over when you were off duty?"

"Right."

"So you would agree it's unusual? For you to pull someone over when you're off duty and on your way home?"

"A little bit, yes."

"So . . . isn't it true you don't always pull people over when you see an infraction?"

"Right. Not always."

"But you pulled my client over because you recognized the car and suspected criminal activity, right?"

Ted asks this nonchalantly, looking down at his pad, not emphasizing that this is the critical question in the case.

Judge Stuber, who has been taking notes even though she has a computer wired to the court reporter's transcription, looks up at the deputy, her pencil poised above her pad for the moment.

"Yes," the deputy answers. "And because of the broken headlamp."

Mike nods, *that's right.*

"Could you look at your report, please?" Ted says. "Second page, third paragraph?"

"Yes, sir." The deputy looks at the report he is tightly clutching in his lap. Mike had the report marked as an exhibit during his preliminary questions, but the deputy has not yet required it because he did his homework and memorized the contents.

"You wrote in your report that you recognized the car from a previous arrest and you suspected criminal activity, possibly related to methamphetamine manufacture."

"Yes, I wrote that."

"And that passage is above the passage where you wrote about the broken headlamp?"

"Yes."

"So you wrote about the suspected criminal activity *before* you added the paragraph about the broken headlamp."

"Right."

"Because the suspected criminal activity, especially since it related to possible methamphetamine manufacture, was more important to you than the broken headlamp?"

"Both were important."

"Okay." This was not the answer Ted hoped for, but he made his point. "Thank you."

"Mr. Lawson," the judge says as Ted sits back down.

Mike stands at counsel table. "Deputy, please look farther down on page two of your report, to the last sentence of the third paragraph."

"Yes," the deputy says, jumping ahead of Mike's next question, "I wrote there that I pulled the defendant over for a broken headlamp that posed a danger on the road."

"Would you have pulled a U-turn and followed the defendant if he didn't have a broken headlamp that posed a danger?"

"No."

"Would you have pulled over the defendant that night for the broken headlamp even if you didn't recognize the car from the previous stop?"

"Yes, I believe so."

Mike was expecting something more definite, but he says, "Thank you," and sits. He is bored with the routine hair splitting, ready for oral argument.

The judge looks over at Ted, who leans back in his chair as though he is going to stand, but then he decides it is too much effort.

"Deputy," he calls out. "You can't say for sure whether or not you would have pulled my client over if you didn't recognize him from the previous stop, can you?"

"For sure? No."

"I'm done."

"Mr. Lawson?"

"Nothing further, Your Honor, thank you."

"Deputy, thank you. You can be seated. Are both parties ready to proceed to argument?"

"Yes, Your Honor."

"Mr. Haller, it's your motion."

Ted stands, holding his brief with both hands.

Howard takes a moment from his note-writing to look back over his shoulder at Porsche, nodding at her reassuringly. Wyatt observes this exchange and feels like strangling him.

"How do you think it went?" the deputy asks Wyatt as he sits down next to him.

Wyatt pats him on the shoulder. "We're probably fucked," he whispers, "but it's not your fault."

"Please proceed," the judge says to Ted, who is still standing, reading his brief.

"*Ladson* is right on point," Ted says, letting the brief drop to his side. "Pretextual stops are unlawful. In *Ladson,* the detectives suspected that the defendant and his partner were involved in drug dealing, so they followed them and pulled them over for expired tabs. Everyone agreed that the tabs on the car were expired, and that's probable cause.

"The problem, the Supreme Court said, was that the officers used the expired tabs as a *pretext* for pulling the vehicle over. A *pretextual* stop. Just like we have here. Everyone agrees that my client's headlight was broken and he could be lawfully pulled over. However, the deputy admitted that he recognized my client's vehicle from a previous contact and that he suspected criminal activity and therefore pulled him over. He's off duty, on his way home, and he isn't going to pull my client over except for the fact that he recognized the car as a tweeker car.

"This is a classic pretextual stop, Your Honor. In *Ladson,* the officers used the expired tabs as an excuse, as a pretext, to pull over someone suspected of drug dealing or something like that, while here the officer used a broken headlamp as an excuse, as a pretext. Right? I mean, that's what happened. Some could say it sounds like good police work, but our Supreme Court has said it's unlawful. So this court has to suppress all the evidence as the fruit of the pretextual stop, as fruit of the poisonous tree."

Ted stands there for a moment, unable to think of anything to add. This is a highly unusual situation—the law is on his side. He savors the self-assurance this inspires and notices that you do not need to pontificate and obfuscate when you are not trying to snooker the court.

Mike, simultaneously, gains an appreciation of the creativity defense attorneys must develop as he prepares to suggest to the court that the law could not or should not mean what it means.

"Mr. Lawson?"

Mike stands and makes eye contact with the judge and he appears confident as he taps into his large capacity for barely justified optimism.

"This case can be distinguished from *Ladson* in three ways, Your Honor. One, in *Ladson* the probable cause for the stop was an expired license. Here, we have a broken headlight that poses a danger on the road in a way that an expired license does not, and therefore cannot be accurately characterized as an excuse, or as a pretext.

"Two, the officers in *Ladson* admitted that their suspicion that one of the occupants was involved in drug dealing was their primary motive for pulling the car over. In fact, they followed the car with the intention of finding a pretext to pull it over. Here, the deputy testified that he noticed the broken headlight even before he recognized the vehicle and suspected possible criminal activity. The broken headlamp, not the suspected criminal activity, was the primary reason for the stop.

"Three, the majority in *Ladson* specifically made note of the fact that the defendants were African-Americans. So either the author of the opinion was making an irrelevant observation, or the court was suggesting that racial profiling was also a factor, a factor that does not exist here."

These distinctions, Mike can tell from the judge's flat demeanor, are not persuading her. She has the expression of imperial disgust trial judges display when they are about to rule in the way they feel they must rather than in the way they would prefer.

"Your Honor," Mike continues, sticking to his scripted argument, despite the unfavorable reception thus far, "on page 843 the court instructs judges to look at the 'totality of the circumstances' in deciding whether or not a stop is pretextual, including, quote, 'the objective reasonableness of the officer's behavior,' unquote. Here the officer's conduct was entirely reasonable, he pulled over a car with a broken headlamp, which posed a danger on a dark and rainy night."

Judge Stuber smiles. "Is objective reasonableness really the test, though, Mr. Lawson? Doesn't *Ladson* require trial courts to consider the subjective intent of the officer? And if the subjective intent is investigation, rather than traffic enforcement, as it was in *Ladson,* and as it appears to be here, doesn't that make for an unlawful stop? Isn't that the opinion of the majority?"

Mike was expecting this, for what it is worth. "In *State v. O'Neill,* 148 Wn.2d 564, a 2003 case, the court backed away from *Ladson,* rejecting a defense argument that the officer's subjective motivation must be considered in weighing reasonableness under article I, section 7. Though *O'Neill* can be distinguished from *Ladson,* it's still significant that the court was unwilling to expand *Ladson* beyond its specific fact pattern."

"I read *O'Neill,*" the judge says, cutting him off, "and in conjunction with *Ladson,* it just confused me. Both were five-four decisions. And Justice Madsen, who wrote the majority opinion in *O'Neill,* wrote the dissent in *Ladson.*" This clearly amuses the judge. "Madsen argued that Justice Sanders, who wrote the majority in *Ladson,* was misstating the issue, misrepresenting legal authority, and basing the majority opinion on false premises."

There is only one answer to this. "Yes, Your Honor."

"That said, I believe *Ladson* is the controlling case here." She puts her hands in the air. "I'm just a trial court judge."

"Yes, but Your Honor, if trial courts follow the reading of *Ladson* that the defense proposes, then it's lawful to pull over a law-abiding citizen for a traffic infraction, but *not* lawful to pull over a suspected criminal for the same infraction. That's so absurd it would make Kafka blush. Therefore, it can't be what the Supreme Court intended. So I'm asking this court to not expand *Ladson* by applying it here. Thank you."

Mike sits, believing more than ever in his position.

"Do you really want to hear anything more from me," Ted asks.

"No."

"I didn't think so."

"Mr. Lawson, you make some good points," the judge says, and Mike knows he has lost. "However, just because something is absurd does not mean it couldn't be what our Supreme Court intended."

Mike has to nod in agreement to this, as does Ted.

"There certainly are some shortcomings in the majority's logic, and some tension between *Ladson* and *O'Neill*, but I believe this raises issues that are more appropriately heard at the appellate level. It is the trial court's duty to follow the law.

"Under our current law if a deputy has a subjective interest in investigating criminal activity, as the deputy here did, but does not have probable cause to pull over a suspect for that criminal activity, but instead pulls the suspect over for a traffic infraction, it's unlawful."

Howard is elbowing Ted excitedly and Ted is whispering back, "*I know, I know.*"

Looking up from her notes, the judge makes eye contact with the young deputy. "Though I may personally think this was good police work, my personal opinions are irrelevant. The Supreme

Court has addressed this issue and I don't have the authority to overturn or ignore the high court. I am therefore granting the defense motion to suppress all the evidence found subsequent to the unlawful stop as fruit of the poisonous tree. . . ."

After a couple of minutes of paperwork formalities, Howard heads back into the gallery, grabs Porsche's hand, and begins quickly stepping out of the courtroom, jumpy from his good fortune, throwing a gloating glance at Wyatt over his shoulder.

"That fuck," Wyatt says as the doors shut behind Howard. "The problem with courtrooms is you can't just shoot people."

Mike gathers his trial notebook and leads Wyatt and the deputy into the hallway.

"Did you guys notice that girl with the defendant," the deputy asks, angry. "She looked like she was about thirteen."

"Of course," Mike says. "The defendant is providing meth to the girl's mother and so she ignores what's going on with her daughter."

"How do you know this?"

"Educated guess after five years in SAU."

"Pretty standard scenario," Wyatt confirms. "Meth," he says, switching into an announcer's voice, "it's not just a drug, it's a lifestyle."

"What are we going to do?" the deputy asks. "This is fucking . . . insane. He's just walking."

Mike and Wyatt exchange a knowing glance, sharing their amusement at the rookie's enthusiasm and naïveté, remembering when they, too, had a sense of outrage.

Wyatt's career choice of cop over lawyer is once again affirmed for him. What Mike could not do in the courtroom, he will have to do in the field. Mike, for his part, has seen the appellate courts reverse convictions for child molesters, rapists, and nearly three hundred murderers with the *Andress* decision, so one meth cook walking is not enough to put him on tilt.

Observing absurdities helps lead to a state of Zen.

"You ready to sign Marvin up?" Wyatt asks. "That was our bet. And now there's this."

Mike nods. "And I'm ready for a drink, too."

"What do you say we push Marvin's assault trial out about four months or so, make Howard his only target, and give him a no-jail deal if he delivers?"

Mike nods again, wondering if he will regret this.

"Who's this Sanders guy you were talking about?" the deputy asks, still baffled and angry.

"That's the problem," Mike says.

"Yep," Wyatt says. "Nobody pays attention to judges."

"Sanders has a power base of right-wing pro-lifers who know nothing about him other than that he's anti-abortion and anti-government," Mike explains to the deputy. "He's like the wacko uncle at the family party, the contrarian who mutters nonsensically and occasionally lashes out, but nobody pays him any attention until he breaks something."

"How did a freak like this get on the Supreme Court?" the deputy asks.

"He was elected."

Mike and Wyatt drive down Sixth Avenue in Mike's eleven-year-old Range Rover, a vehicle that has oddly become the preferred ride for Pacific Northwest drug dealers. They pass House of Records, Shakabrah, Jazzbones, and various new businesses cropping up in the gentrifying neighborhood.

Hell's Kitchen, façade bright red, stands out among the storefronts. They park just beyond the club by Rocket Records, across from the West End Pub and Grill. Smokers linger in front of the bars, relegated outside by the smoking ban and undeterred by the drizzle. Wispy trails of nicotine mix with breath clouds. Mike would join them, but his thrist for alcohol trumps his desire for nicotine.

Mike and Wyatt enter Hell's Kitchen and there is no music and half of the beer-stained pool tables are unused and the crowd is sparse, which surprises them.

"You said Vicci Martinez was playing tonight?"

"I thought it was tonight," Wyatt says. "Suki told me a while back."

A Tacoma singer, guitarist, and *Star Search* finalist, Martinez usually draws large crowds to local venues. Something is therefore amiss.

Wyatt consults the bartender and learns that Martinez is next week and tonight a poetry slam is about to begin.

"Fuck me," Wyatt says to Mike.

"Should we go to the Parkway?" Mike suggests.

"No, I need hard liquor. Now."

Mike orders two scotches and two Budweisers and the scotch arrives promptly and strong. Buds follow, served in plastic cups.

Behind the bartender is a poster of Stacy Fuson, the St. Pauli beer girl from Tacoma, posing in a red skirt and a black and white top that is a cross between traditional Bavarian wear and a Victoria's Secret bustier. Her blond hair flows down to her breasts where the ends curl like fingers, her mouth is slightly open in a come-hither expression, and one hand rests on her bare hip while the other holds out a tray with three green bottles of St. Pauli beer.

"Do you think Stacy ever comes back to Tacoma?"

"You can take the girl out of Tacoma," Wyatt says, "but you can't take Tacoma out of the girl."

"Does Neko Case still live here?"

"The singer? I don't think so."

"Some good musicians come from Tacoma," Mike says, sipping his cheap scotch before he realizes it is better suited for gulping. "Have you ever heard Leonard Cohen's song, 'Tacoma Trailer'?"

"No."

"It's an instrumental. Cool song."

"Too bad he's famous for his lyrics."

"And for being with beautiful women. Including Rebecca DeMornay."

"That's impressive, especially since the guy looks like a basset hound."

"He's an artist." Mike shrugs. "I have to tell you, Suki is the best looking and coolest woman I've ever seen you with."

"Thanks for mentioning that. She moved out last week."

"No shit?"

"No shit."

"How did that happen?"

Wyatt shrugs. "How do these things ever happen?"

"The guy fucks up?"

"She quoted *Annie Hall,* the line about how a relationship is like a shark—if it doesn't keep moving, it dies."

"You should have never turned her on to Woody Allen."

"She loves funny movies. Best line in *Annie Hall*?"

"'I have to go now, Duane, because I'm due back on planet Earth.'"

"'Don't knock masturbation. It's sex with someone I love.'" Wyatt polishes off the house scotch with a grimace. "I can't believe she moved out."

"You blew it," Mike says, then orders another round.

"No argument on that point from me, Counselor."

"We need a new plan."

"For Howard, or my love life?"

"Both."

"I have definitely not reached a state of Zen on this case."

"Neither have I."

"Okay." Wyatt takes a long sip of his beer. "I have a confession to make."

"Yeah?"

"I always kind of liked Bill Clinton."

"That's your idea of a confession?"

"You know what he should have done? When everyone was nipping at his heels he should have just said, 'Yeah, I smoked some pot in college, yeah, I banged a few gals in trailer parks, and yeah, I got a blow job in the Oval Office, but most of the time I was *working my ass off for all of you.* Now, let me get back to work.'"

"Where were you when he needed you?"

Wyatt shrugs. "He should have called."

Fresh drinks in hand, they leave the bar for the dark and small band room on the west side of the club. Onstage, under a single unsteady spotlight, a middle-aged man with thinning hair and tinted wire-rimmed glasses introduces himself as Apple Seattle and begins an adjective-laden poem about a suicidal poet.

He says "famous poets" with no hint of irony and the audience stares up at him as though he is a misshapen zoo animal.

"You suck," a guy in a stocking cap yells.

"Seattle sucks," a woman adds.

As a young teenager Mike often took the bus to Seattle for rock shows, catching national acts as well as Seattle bands like the Fastbacks and Tacoma bands like Girl Trouble, but lately even the staid *Seattle Weekly* has taken to calling its namesake city "Nanny-town" because of the clampdown on smokers and strippers and music clubs. Mike used to blame the poseurs who flocked to Seattle in the boom years, though truth be told Seattle was never as grungy as Aberdeen, Olympia, Spanaway, or Tacoma.

As the crowd static rises, Apple Seattle moves his mouth closer to the microphone, carefully enunciating "precious" and "ponder" and other *p* words that pop as the heckling continues.

"That's it," Wyatt says.

"What?"

"We've got to welcome him to Pierce County."

"Who? The clown on the stage?"

"No, Howard. I think it's time to show him some true Pierce County grit. Maybe even turn Marcello loose on him."

"This does not sound good."

"We've been too easygoing, playing nice, playing by the rules."

"We have to play by the rules."

Suddenly a cup of beer is launched from just left of Wyatt. As the projectile enters the glare of the spotlight the poet spots it, but he freezes and the cup explodes on his chest, cascading beer over his surprised face.

This inspires applause and hearty cheers.

"Welcome to Tacoma!"

"What the hell is wrong with you people?" the contestant asks, wiping beer from his glasses, dripping.

"You're pretentious!"

"You blow!"

"Loser!"

Mike turns to Wyatt. "We're going to have to leave, or you're going to have to arrest someone."

"'Forget it, Jake,'" Wyatt says, slipping into a vaguely recognizable Jack Nicholson imitation, "it's T-Town."

THE INFORMATION AGE

yr free nothin has meaning u will rule
no way
out no way to escape yrself u have
no control
of yr mind u cannot stop yr thoughts
they pour
in from the world they well up inside they whisper
they lie
yr mind will destroy u it produces
uncontrolled urges
to whatever u will rule the known world
rule all
dream of power of money of genius u will be famous
u will
know the gutter the want the the

Howard suddenly stops typing midsentence, his fingertips wet and slippery and momentarily disconnected from his brain, which has suddenly been seized by a need for information.

He minimizes the tweeker blog window, brings up LINX instead, glancing over his shoulder to make sure the other patrons are not watching. Bertolino's, a twenty-four-hour Internet coffee shop near the University of Puget Sound, is a frequent late-night haunt of his. The 77s play on the house stereo and the crowd mostly consists of college and high school kids playing chess, staring at their laptops, and chatting across old wooden tables. Nobody appears to be paying attention to him.

LINX, the Legal Information Network Exchange, available to all at the Pierce County Web site, lists court dates for defendants. Howard, like most other cooks and dealers, tracks tweeker cases and when he sees a court date set out unusually far, as Marvin's Assault One trial has been, it serves as a warning that the defendant might be working the beef off as an informant. Suspicions confirmed, and unable to concentrate on a single task long, he clicks the blog back up and begins typing again, continuing to cut and paste as he riffs on the entries of other tweekers.

u will
die in the gutter u will do or be none of it
sweet revenge
demands that u even the scores first and last
betrayal is
the lowest low of the lower lowest lowdown
snitches suck
u long
to stop yr mind but u cannot stop nothin
yr mind
is in constant turmoyle and it rules doesn't rule
it lies
u long to be loved but u hate those u long
to love
u long to destroy those u love u love those u destroy
no control
u know what u are doing but not why u do it
u decide
that u will do one thing and then do the other
u drive
to do what u will never understand u think but

u remain
outside yr thoughts u act but yr actions
mean nothin
u place yrself in situations that will cause u mental
and physical
harm but u deny the harm it does even tho u know
cannot stop
moving u cannot stop time everything is unbearable
everything is
the empty nothing that is life the known
empty ness
reminds u constantly of the possibility of being
filled up
yet if it existed completely then u would have no need
to exist
u will never change u enjoy it for u need pain like
u need
pleasure they both give u a glimpse of the infinite
they release
u from life by intensity to the extreme so that u
no longer
exist within u scream u beat yr body
u feel
pity for yrself as u hollow in self satisfied
self hatred
in dreams u think are forever u think u are
special different
u are nothing u are human u are worthless u will
never change
porsche is fast as the white lines gone
white skin

powder and ice u are my life and my wife
tweaking forever
u will never die u will die slowly as the world ends
but death
will not save u there is no way out there is no
hope here

Howard strolls through the Sears at the Tacoma Mall looking for the chainsaw section, humming "Kill You," the Eminem song he heard on Joe's boom box that gave him the idea.

He has been up for three days and he is jerking like a marionette and none of the floor people have offered to help him, which he is completely okay with. So far he has stolen lithium batteries, a pocket knife, and pliers, just because he can. His pockets are bulging and he feels invincible.

One of the best ways to increase your cachet as a drug dealer is to beat the System, *beat the Man,* and Howard enjoys his resulting status. In the last few years he has been charged with meth-related crimes three times and three times the charges have been dismissed.

Such news spreads quickly in Methlehem.

"I'm bulletproof," is what he likes to say by way of explanation, sometimes implying that he is so heavily connected the prosecutor made the cases disappear.

While the cops and prosecutors hammer the stupider cooks, sending them away with double-digit sentences, Howard's stature and sales increase proportionally. He believes he is the only major local cook competing successfully with the Mexicans.

This, in his mind, is why the Mexicans have been trying to recruit someone to snitch him out—they want to eliminate the competition because they cannot match his product. He is convinced that the Mexicans were somehow behind his recent arrest. This is how it is done in the drug world: dealers wipe out other dealers by having one of their clients turn snitch and let the cops do the work.

After several minutes of confused wandering, he spots a yellow chainsaw displayed on top of a stack of boxes. He does not like the yellow, it strikes him as too sissy, but a black and red one nearby appeals to him. Electric, the box says, which conjures up visions of lightning bolts for him.

Though the woman at the checkout counter appears nervous, she accepts his stolen VISA card with no questions and he walks out with a sixteen-inch 3.5-horsepower Craftsman chainsaw with "vibration neutralizing technology" and a twenty-foot extension cord.

"Would you ever live with a cat?" June asks.

Mike has no idea where this question is coming from.

June is sipping a Manhattan on the couch, the martini glass held just below her chin, the red cherry magnified at the bottom of the amber liquid. She is wearing a black evening dress and cat-eye glasses.

"No," he admits, on the couch beside her, scotch in hand.

June's studio apartment is suggestive of a mild obsessive-compulsive disorder: books are alphabetized in a tall Plexiglas bookcase and broken into categories, fiction, nonfiction, hardbacks, mass-market paperbacks, and trade paperbacks; Almond, Bushnell, Coupland, Fitzgerald, Janowitz, McInerney, Minot, Pasternak, Rust, Stein, Susann, Tartt, Vonnegut, and so on. Magazines—*Vogue, Glamour, Pages, The New Yorker*—are laid over each other in a perfect fan shape and there is not a CD, DVD, or knickknack in sight, only a white iPod. Her hardwood floors are polished, the pink and green throw rug appears freshly vacuumed, and the couch and two chairs are perched on the rug at perfect angles to each other.

Mike is put in mind of a showroom.

"I don't want to freak you out," June says, "since we've only been dating three and three-quarter months, but I just want to know where you stand on the cat question."

He nods and sets his scotch on the square coaster on the wooden coffee table, twirling the coaster slightly. June reaches out and moves the coaster so the sides are parallel to the table edges again.

Mike does not remember her doing this at the Swiss, or 21 Commerce, or anywhere else they have been drinking, and he is sure he would remember. As a test, he takes another long pull of his drink and sets it down again, twirling the coaster again.

"I don't know how anyone could live with a cat," June says, eyeing his askew coaster.

"I wouldn't want to," Mike says, "but I can see how someone else might find it . . . possible."

"They defecate in the house."

"I think they use kitty litter boxes."

"Which are inside the house."

"True."

"I was dating this one guy, and he told me he was a cat lover." Unable to take it any longer, June adjusts the coaster again. "What kind of guy is a cat lover?"

"I don't know."

"I told him I couldn't live with a cat unless the cat stayed outside. He said his cat was an indoor cat, so I suggested the cat could live in a cat shed."

"A cat shed?"

"Like a toolshed," June says, tapping a finger with a red-painted nail against her cheekbone, "but you put cats in it instead of tools."

"Of course."

"And he answered that the shed would be outside and so it would be like putting the cat outside and I said it's not outside if the cat is *inside* the cat shed. He repeated that the cat shed itself was outside, and I said, yeah, well, a house is outside, too, but if the cat is inside the house the cat isn't outside, is it?" June smiles like a lawyer who has just made her case. "Don't you agree that if a cat is in a cat shed he's inside, not outside?"

Mike wonders if everyone he knows is nuts.

"Well," June says, "isn't that true?"

Funny how normal she seemed in other environments, Mike thinks. Here, in her natural habitat, disorders he cannot quite identify are freely emerging.

"Absolutely," Mike answers, wanting to get the hell away from this subject. "How did your paper comparing Vonnegut and Jacqueline Susann work out?"

"The professor gave it an A." June shrugs. "He says I'm an 'astonishing' writer. But maybe he says I'm that because he wants to sleep with me?"

"Maybe he wants to sleep with you because he thinks you're an astonishing writer."

This elicits a smile. "Yeah, you think so?"

"I do."

"I hadn't thought of it that way." June finishes her Manhattan, then delicately fishes the cherry out and sucks it off the stem into her mouth. "I was worried you were going to have to cancel again tonight, since you're so busy here in crime city USA, and I'd have to eat alone."

"Well, I'm glad I'm here."

This is true. He is not willing to rule her out as a marital possibility just because of her eccentricities, especially given her tolerance of his own quirks.

"Me, too. And I'm glad you don't mind vegan stuff."

He does, but not too much. Again he takes a sip of his drink and sets his glass down so it twirls the coaster slightly. Again, June squares the angles. He is starting to find this strangely charming.

"You never answered about the cat, though," she says.

"What part?"

"You don't want to live with a cat? Do you?"

"No."

"Good. Everyone has their idiosyncrasies, their carnival desires and so on, but I couldn't have a future with a guy who liked cats. So maybe we have a future."

Mike nods. "I'd like to read one of your stories."

"I just finished one about a girl stalking Robert Downey, Jr."

"Cool."

"Maybe I'll write one about you."

"I've always wanted to be immortal."

"You don't think it would get boring?"

TRUST

Marvin sucks in the white smoke as he holds the lighter under the bulb of the meth pipe and for a brief moment he remembers that he has a urine test scheduled tomorrow as part of the pretrial release conditions, but no matter. Missed urine tests are customarily without consequences.

Though Marvin is still facing potential prison time for "the unfortunate accident," as his attorney calls the shooting, he feels confident he can fulfill his deal with Wyatt and the prosecutor and thereby stay free. While he is working for *the Man,* he is also working for the other man, Howard, delivering one-ounce baggies stamped with Howard's Superman logo.

He is sharing part of a recent delivery with the customers at a double-wide trailer when the door is kicked open, aluminum snapping and glass breaking.

In steps Howard with a chainsaw in one hand and a long extension cord in the other.

"Holy fuck shit," the resident tweeker says.

Marvin stands, while the other tweekers stay seated in front of a television, two playing with Xbox controllers, one disassembling a controller and wearing a Bates Technical College sweatshirt, all craning their necks to stare at Howard as he kicks his way through the trash piled on the floor, the empty cans, ashtrays, clothes, mason jars, stolen car stereos, and porn magazines.

A cat dashes out past the broken door.

"Howard," Marvin says.

"So you're Howard," the resident finally says, pausing the video game, Grand Theft Auto. "What's going on, man?"

"You shut the fuck up," Howard answers.

Finding an outlet, Howard plugs in the chainsaw and turns it on and revs it up into a menacing whine. Nobody moves. Raindrops echo off the metal roof of the trailer and this is the only sound left in the room when Howard eases the trigger back off.

"Hello, Marvin," Howard says. "Sit down on the couch over there."

"I—I was bringing you the money," Marvin stutters, sitting. "I was just having one hit first."

"I know you were bringing me the money."

"Well, then . . . what is the . . ."

"The problem?"

"Right, yes."

"The problem is that there's been a lot of snitching going on. And nobody is going to fucking snitch on me."

"No snitches here," one of the video gamers says.

"*You,*" Howard says, "sit down and shut the fuck up."

Already sitting, the gamers decide to stay that way.

"So Marvin," Howard says, turning back to him, stepping closer. "Looks like your case was set out several months."

"LINX?"

Howard nods. "Why, Marvin?"

Marvin, who has been to the paranoid abyss on many meth runs, recognizes exactly where Howard is—the madness, the anger, the voices—and it scares the holy hell out of him. He tries on Howard what people have tried on him when he was out of his mind: calm reasoning.

"You know you can trust me, right, Howard?"

"Can I trust you, Marvin?"

"Yes, yes, of course."

Howard revs the chainsaw back up. "I can trust you? over the rising whine.

"Yes, you know you can." Sweat is running down M greasy face as he suddenly remembers that reasoning has worked on him or any other tweeker at a time like this. "P you know you can trust me."

"I know that?"

"You do, yes."

"Question is, though, do you trust me?"

"Yes, yes!"

"Good, Marvin. Good. That's the right answer."

Marvin exhales loudly, and his body sinks back into the couch, but his eyes stay on the chainsaw as it suddenly lashes out—Howard rapidly and crazily sweeps it back and forth over the coffee table, knocking off beer cans, cigarettes, and makeshift ashtrays, and the crashing sounds mix with the screech of the chainsaw.

"Fuck," Marvin yells, his voice weak in the face of the chainsaw's volume.

Howard swings the chainsaw up over his head like a samurai's sword. He lets the engine wind down as he stares at Marvin and after a few seconds the room is utterly quiet again except for the echoing rain.

"Please," Marvin says.

"Have you ever read Nietzsche?" Howard asks.

"Who?"

"Why must I live my life surrounded by morons?" Howard asks the ceiling, then gazes down again at Marvin. "Have you read *Mein Kampf*?"

"No."

"Do you know what it is?"

"No."

"It's probably the greatest book ever written."

"Who wrote it?" Marvin says, desperately trying to participate in the conversation, to act as though everything is normal, to *maintain*. "That guy, Nietzsche?"

"You fucking moron. *Hitler* wrote it."

Howard's eyes bore into his employee with such ferocity it causes Marvin's hands to start shaking in his lap, fingers twitching like he is playing the piano.

"Hitler says a man can't serve two masters," Howard says, still holding the chainsaw steady over his head.

"Hitler says." Marvin nods.

"Will you serve me, Marvin?"

"Yes, yes."

"Do you trust me?"

"Yes."

"You have to trust me to serve me."

"Yes, I do, I do."

"Put a finger out on the coffee table."

"What?

"Put a fucking finger on the coffee table."

"What . . . finger?"

"What finger? I don't care! Your fucking forefinger!"

"My forefinger?" Marvin examines his hands, trying to remember which finger is his forefinger, trying to avoid thinking about what is happening.

"The one next to your thumb, moron!"

"The one next to my thumb."

"Put it out on the coffee table. Now!"

Marvin complies, moving in slow motion except for the shaking finger. He watches it twitch on the table as though it has no connection to him.

"Close your eyes."

Marvin squeezes them shut, *it's just a test, it's just a test, it's just a test . . .*

Still frozen on the floor in front of the television, open-mouthed, the gamers stare at Howard. The reality of the rattling chainsaw is no more or no less engaging to them than the mondo-violence of the video games, but the sound effect is quite impressive.

Stepping to the side, focusing on the finger, Howard brings the chainsaw down like a guillotine, pulling the trigger as he does. The whishing saw teeth cut through Marvin's finger and the table in a flash, blood and sawdust and bone erupt into the air in a red and yellow mist.

Snapping open his eyes, Marvin quickly brings his hand up to his face. Blood pumps out of his jagged finger nub in rhythm with his rapidly beating heart and pours in bright red streams down his palm from where his knuckle used to be and all he can think is, *How did I get here?*

Flames in the natural gas fireplace flicker over the ceramic logs and only a couple customers remain, both reading on the leather couches near the fire. Suki does not mind working at Cutter's Point on weeknights like this.

She sits on a stool behind the mahogany counter and reads the book Wyatt gave her before they broke up, *A Wild Sheep Chase*. Because the book is a detective novel of sorts, and the lead character is not unlike Wyatt in some ways, she wonders if he gave it to her as something to remind her of him.

If so, it works.

Though she left Foxes on her own, she partially credits Wyatt. He gave her confidence and he helped her to realize that she overvalued money. When she was eighteen and ambitious and new to dancing she could make hundreds of dollars in a night and that seemed important.

Her promise to herself was that she would not get old in the club. Old, however, is a relative term. When she was eighteen she thought twenty-two was old, but now that she's twenty-six she thinks twenty-two was young but twenty-six is not quite old and, therefore, she kept her promise.

Unable to concentrate on her book, she begins cleaning up. As she is wiping cup circles from the polished bar, the front door swings open and cold air rushes in along with a thin blond man wearing jeans and a burgundy Washington State Cougars sweatshirt. He tracks in dead wet maple leaves with his cowboy boots.

Instantly she does not like his vibe, her creep radar going off as it did so many times at Foxes, *tweeker*. Because of their constant need for stimulation, tweekers often visit strip clubs when they are not busy stocking up on porn videos and sex toys from the Castle Superstore.

"Can I help you?" she asks as he approaches.

"You're Suki, right?"

"Who are you?"

"Duchess told me you were working here now. Duchess from Foxes. The Filipina girl."

"Yes, I know Duchess." And the man before her does not, Suki assumes, or he would not be referring to Alexis by her stage name.

"Do you know who I am?" Howard asks.

"No."

"Your boyfriend does."

"He knows lots of people." She wonders if telling this tweeker creep that Wyatt is no longer her boyfriend would make him go away. "That's his job."

"Yeah, and it's my job, too. I'm Howard Schultz." When Suki keeps her poker face, he adds, "Your boyfriend knows me as the King of Methlehem."

"What would you like to order, Mr. Schultz?"

"I just want you to tell your boyfriend that I know he's looking for me, and I'm waiting for him to figure it out. Can you handle that message?"

"I'm going to have to ask you to leave now."

He laughs, flashing tweeker teeth. "I'm already gone, hon, already gone."

Before he is even out of the door Suki is on her cell phone, calling Wyatt, hoping he is home in his loft just above the shop. She hangs up when he does not answer.

Into the back of the former milk van thirteen Pierce County officers file in order, taking bench seats in the cargo section, facing each other. Each of them is dressed in black boots, dark canvas jumpsuits, and Kevlar vests. SHERIFF is written across their chests in large yellow letters. Assault rifles are in hand or slung over their shoulders, Glocks hang in hip holsters.

As the unmarked van drives at the pace of traffic from their headquarters toward the area between Roy and Eatonville where Howard is reportedly operating a lab, enough testosterone runs through the men to field a professional sports team.

Wyatt reviews a map of the area while he talks on a headset to a deputy who is positioned on a hill above the property, reconnoitering through a light morning haze that glows in the low sun of winter. When the clouds part and the sun brightens the landscape, the beauty of the Northwest is stunning.

"It's a good day," the deputy reports, "clear view, but the only action I've seen is one man moving something from a shed or barn to the main house."

A good day—the line calls to Wyatt's mind a quote from "Little Big Man" where Chief Dan George says, "It's a good day to die."

"Was he armed?" Wyatt asks.

"Not that I could see."

"Blue tarps?"

"Roger that."

A few minutes later the word is given to suit up and the officers don breathing masks with glass visors and dark metal helmets, prepared as always for the worst.

The van turns up the dirt driveway, passing piles of garbage and hulks of rusted cars. Three Harleys rest on kickstands near the front door of the main residence, and the van stops just short of knocking over the bikes.

As soon as the engine shuts down the back doors swing open, and the officers jump out in twos, all scrambling as fast as they can in the bulky outfits. Four run for the shed, four run around to the back of the house, and five approach the front door, Marcello carrying a steel battering ram with MEET MY LITTLE FRIEND written on the side.

"Open the door, Sheriff's Department, police," the driver of the van announces over a loudspeaker, adding "police" because "Sheriff's Department" may not mean anything to non-English-speaking residents.

Within seconds of the command, Marcello breaks in the front door and the officers fan out into the main room, weapons ready. They can hear loud hip-hop music vibrating through their masks and helmets. In front of them is a couch, a television with a porn movie playing, girl-on-girl at the moment, plywood tables on sawhorses, laboratory-quality heating elements, beakers with bubbling red liquid, and huge buckets full of white powder. The plasterboard walls bleed with red stains.

Red Phosphorous lab, Wyatt notes, *not Howard's style.*

Just then three bulky men in black leather riding outfits and red-stained surgical masks rumble into the main room from the kitchen area—one has a shotgun and the other two have handguns. Shock shows on their faces and they stop at the threshold when they realize they are facing officers with leveled assault rifles.

Two of the three bikers facing the officers drop their guns and raise their hands and the officers momentarily restrain the trigger fingers, but the one with the shotgun fires a single blast.

Inside the house the sound is deafening.

Wyatt takes the shot in his chest and is knocked onto his back, breath expelling, but it is only birdshot and most of the pellets are picked up by the Kevlar vest. A few feet behind him glass beakers shatter and toxic chemicals run onto the floor with a splash and a hiss.

All of the other officers instantly return fire and in less than five seconds the man with the shotgun takes eleven hits—two in the face, five in the chest, three in the legs, one in the crotch—and he backs into a wall and slides down dead, but another twenty-some bullets miss. Two of the off-mark bullets hit the bulkiest biker in his stomach, causing him to drop his hands and fall and curl. Blood from their two bodies mixes on the dirty linoleum floor.

When the shooting stops there is stillness except for the wounded biker's moans and the voice of the unscathed biker, who keeps repeating, *"Llena de gracia."*

"He just kept saying, 'Full of grace,' " Marcello, a stocky young officer with a goatee, relates. "In Spanish."

"What do you suppose that means?" another asks.

"Full of grace?"

"No, that he was using Spanish?"

"How about that he knows Spanish?"

"But the Mexicans and the bikers don't usually work together."

"Yeah, I'm not sure what the hell happened out there."

"I wonder if they're working together now."

"They're competitors."

"Mexicans don't cook here, they ship it in."

"I wouldn't read too much into it," Wyatt says from the hospital bed. "The guy just happened to be a Hispanic biker. It's not a global alliance."

St. Joseph Medical Center sits on a hill overlooking downtown and the tide flats, a large white cross glowing on the east side of the building. Through a single oval window at the end of the room Wyatt can see the city lights glitter and he can pick out where he lives, the home he will be away from for tonight. White bandages are crisscrossed over his chest and neck, covering the holes pellets were removed from.

There will be other methamphetamine-related casualties later tonight—almost a quarter of the hospital's Emergency Room admissions are related to methamphetamine in some way: burns, assaults, domestic violence, child abuse, and twentysomethings with strokes.

Ten milligrams of Vicodin is all the painkiller Wyatt rated, and he is a little disappointed. He would like to light up a joint, but he figures his crew would not go for that and neither would the hospital staff, who have already let them stay beyond visiting hours. A group of men with guns and badges are often granted privileges, even when they are in plainclothes and look like a grunge band with their ragged pants, flannel shirts, and facial hair.

Though Wyatt sometimes feels old around them, he appreciates his crew's presence, their camaraderie. One of the things about being a cop is that you always have your crew, someone watching your back, and for this he is grateful. He would not want to be among those that go through life with their back unguarded, nor would he want to rely on Byzantine alliances as Mike does in the prosecutor's office. Mike tells his trial unit to be mutually respectful, but *they're lawyers* and Wyatt thinks this is like telling porcupines to play nice.

Just when it feels like his crew's antics might be winding down and he might have time to think, to plot, their sergeant enters the room. He is almost fifty, just a few years from retirement, wearing baggy jeans and a USC baseball cap.

"Nice shooting, guys," he says, the sarcasm instantly obvious. "Looks like you got off about thirty-five rounds and hit the target eleven times. Not even a one-in-three ratio, unless you want to count the two that hit the dumb fucker who had his hands in the air." He laughs and shakes his head. "From about ten fucking feet away."

"It was more like eleven feet."

"Yeah, yeah," the sergeant says, stepping over to Wyatt. "So what the hell happened to you?"

As soon as Wyatt saw the Red P equipment, he knew it was not Howard's lab.

Marvin lied. The fuck.

Later, in the ambulance, Wyatt figured that Howard used

Marvin to set him up. He expects the idea was that he would take out the biker rivals, and the shooting was just a bonus.

"I forgot to duck," Wyatt says, stealing the Ronald Reagan line.

"You make me look bad when you get shot."

"It's a buzz-killer, too," Marcello adds.

In 1995 the sergeant was part of a drug raid where a small-time dealer, Brian Eggleston, murdered Pierce County Sheriff's Deputy John Bananola during a gunfight by holding a .45 to the wounded officer's head and executing him. Eggleston, bleeding from five bullet wounds, including one in his testicles, thought he was dying and wanted to take the officer with him. To everyone's surprise, Eggleston lived. His survival resulted in three costly trials—the first two were reversed on appeal—and ultimately a thirty-eight-year sentence. The sergeant knows that any raid can end in the death of an officer and he is relieved that this one did not and so he is in a good mood.

"We're going to have to charge you for the vest," the sergeant says. "And the breathing mask. So you'll be going without for a while. County's cheap, you know."

"Did the other guy live?" Wyatt asks.

"The dumb fucker with his hands in the air. Yeah, he'll live."

"I want to talk to him."

"He's at Tacoma General. We already talked. Got the whole story from him and the full-of-grace guy."

"Bikers?"

"Yeah, not Howard's."

"I figured."

"So what happened here?"

"Not sure yet." He does not want to share it yet.

"You're too focused on this one target when there's plenty of other vermin in the sea."

"Vermin in the sea?"

"You know what I mean. You're taking a break."

"I wanna take a break, too," one of his crew says.

"Me, too."

"Do I have to get shot?"

And the ribbing begins again until the door opens and Mike Lawson enters, in a suit with his tie loosened, direct from the courthouse.

"Guess they'll let anyone in here," the sergeant says.

"Heard about the shoot-out," Mike says. "You guys get all the fun. Hey, Wyatt."

"Hey, chief."

"Wyatt's taking a break for a while," the sergeant tells Mike.

"Is that right, Wyatt?"

"Sure."

Mike can tell by Wyatt's deadpan expression that there will be no break.

"So, Mike, you running for prosecutor next year?" one of the crew asks. "You here looking for votes?"

"Yeah, I can't have reliable votes dying on me."

"Don't worry, I'll vote for you. And so will my girlfriend."

"She would have to be eighteen," Mike says, provoking a few knowing laughs.

Mike hates hospitals—everything about them reminds him of death: the smell, the equipment, the white jackets on the staff. He wants to ask Wyatt if he felt the closeness of death in the gunfire and if it panicked him or calmed him. Did he find Zen in the concentrated moment? This, however, is not the time.

Know your audience.

"We'll charge the cooks up in custody tomorrow morning," Mike says. "Except the dead one you guys used for target practice."

"You're going to let the dead guy skate?" the sergeant says with mock indignation, and his crew jumps on this.

"Another criminal gets off on a technicality."

"Lawyers are such pussies."

"Be careful, Wyatt's a lawyer."

"No, he's a cop with a law degree."

"Which is like a bear with a bicycle."

Mike admires their ability to channel their fear of death into laughter. He tries to imagine how weird it would have been if Wyatt died, to test the degree of grief, if only for a few seconds.

"If I die suddenly," Wyatt says, spooking Mike as he taps into his thoughts, "I'm going to come back for an official good-bye. You'll see a gray feather floating in your face and that feather, Counselor, will be me."

"A feather. Me, too. What kind of drugs did they give you?"

Two nights after the shooting, Wyatt is home.

He lies in bed staring out at the fog covering the tide flats, the mist thick right up to the loft windows, obliterating the lights and cranes of the port. Albers Mill Lofts, bordering the waterway, about a hundred yards out, appear only as a dark shadow in the haze. Pugnetti Park, even closer, is visible only as a few tree branches that seem to float unconnected in the air.

Every ten minutes the LINK, a light-rail streetcar, buzzes by and he hears the clanking on the track and the hum of the electric engines.

Though he was told the Vicodin would help him sleep, it gives him a buzz as it mixes with his adrenaline and he does not want to fall asleep and waste the high. As Winston Churchill once noted, there is nothing more exhilarating than to be shot at unsuccessfully.

He wants to plan for his next move, avenge the setup, but instead he devises a plan for victory in Iraq. Let the Sunnis and Shiites go berserk, and while they're slaughtering each other and babbling about jihad and virgins, our troops just quietly exit stage left, like characters in a *Seinfeld* episode. As for Iran, just lock up the short guy with the hobo beard, Ahmanutjob, and the world will be safer.

Shouldn't follow the news, bad for the head.

When Wyatt hears a knock, and then his front door creeps open, his hand instantly goes for his gun. He finds skin instead.

"Wyatt," Suki says as she enters, "it's me. Mike told me what happened."

He turns his head slowly, but his neck hurts so he cannot bring himself around.

"I hope I didn't wake you," she says, stepping into his line of sight, carrying a coffee cup. "But I was worried." She reaches out and holds his hand. "Are you okay?"

"Fine, just can't sleep."

"I knew you'd be awake. You're a bad sleeper."

"I didn't realize you still had a key."

"I've been meaning to return it."

"No worries. Where did you move?"

"For a few days I lived with a friend near King's Books, but pretty quickly I found an apartment near Starbucks, the one by the Spar, so I'm still not far away. I thought about Gig Harbor, but couldn't afford it."

"Gig Harbor? That's where Charles Johnson lives."

"Who?"

"The accidental Supreme Court Justice. Didn't actually campaign for the job, but voters liked the name."

"Nice name."

"Yeah, nice guy, too, except he signed off on the *Andress* decision along with that schizo Barbara Madsen, the case that reversed the convictions of almost three hundred murderers, mostly wife beaters and child abusers."

Suki frowns. "Could we talk about something else?"

"Sorry."

"You're too focused on all the crap that's wrong in the world. You know that, right?"

"I know, I'm sorry. How have you been doing?"

"Good, working at the coffee shop mostly."

"How about school?"

"I'm getting together my application for the UW."

"Good."

Glancing around, she says, "Your loft feels even more vacant than usual. How are *you* doing?"

"Fine."

"Fine except you were shot."

"The vest caught most of it." He squeezes her hand, needing the sense of something solid. "I've missed you."

"I've missed you, too." She smiles. "Are you stoned?"

"Vicodin is all."

"No pot?"

"No."

"Good. Pot's not sexy, not for a forty-year-old."

This hits Wyatt hard. "Seriously?"

"Part of your appeal is that you're this strong, upstanding, together adult. Not Tommy Chong."

"Now you tell me."

"I wanted to tell you before, but I didn't want to do it just after moving in."

"Why not?"

"For the same reason you didn't want to tell me to quit dancing. We didn't want to butt into each other's lives too much. But now I can say it as your friend."

"You okay with the Vicodin?"

"Anytime you're shot." Suki smiles. "So how did it happen?"

"Long story."

"You trying to be a hero?"

"No. Todd Beamer is a hero, Pat Tillman is a hero. I'm just trying to clean up one speck of evil."

"I have to tell you something."

"Okay."

"Howard came into the coffee shop and tried to talk to me and he said for me to tell you that he said that he was waiting for you or something and I was thinking it didn't mean anything," she says, rapidly, apologetically, "but I called you anyway, but you weren't there, so I never called back and I was still mad at you and I didn't really want to talk and I didn't know what it meant anyway and—"

"Hey, hey, relax, don't worry about it."

"You're not understanding me," she says, catching her breath.

"I get it. Howard came into the coffee shop and said something about how he was waiting for me. Right?"

"Right."

"But he wasn't there when I was shot."

"No?"

"No, I wasn't shot by Howard."

"Who, then?"

"You know what? You're exhausting me."

This makes her laugh. "Yeah, I guess I was always good at that."

"Yeah."

"Usually not with words."

"Sometimes with words."

"I didn't want to break up, you know."

"Then why did you?"

"Fuck." She sighs. "Why are men so stupid?"

"That question is out of my jurisdiction."

"Even Mike thinks you're obsessed with Howard."

"Hey, he's trying to get me killed."

"So you're going to keep chasing him until he succeeds?"

"Howard's a tweeker, he'll stumble at some point."

"So . . . if you kill the king, does that make you the king?"

"Did Mike say that?"

"I'm asking you."

"Mike's eyeing the crown, not me."

"Men." Suki shakes her head. "What's wrong with all of you?"

Wyatt's Vicodin-addled brain slowly considers this, flashing on images of elementary school, Little League sports, toy soldiers, sex, poker, apes, war, the opening scene of *2001: A Space Odyssey,* and Rebecca DeMornay and the train set in *Risky Business,* before deducing the rhetorical nature of the question.

"You look good," he says. "Your hair's shorter."

"I needed a change, I guess."

"Well, it looks good. You really look good."

He means it and she knows him well enough to feel this. They stare at each other for a long beat, both aware of the physical attraction, both aware of something additional, too.

"Well, thanks," she says softly. "It may be the last haircut I can afford for a while."

"You haven't gone back to the club?"

"It took me longer than it should have to get out of there, but sometimes it takes a while to do something even when we know we should. You don't really know something until you act on it, right?"

He nods in agreement, mind and eyes wandering.

Condensation drips down the tall windows, increasing the blurriness and otherworldliness of the tableau. Fog, snow, rain, sun, any weather change appeals to Wyatt. Murders, robberies, beatings, even full-on disasters, these, too, have an appeal for the exhilaration they can provide. He sometimes worries that he is hooked on the unhealthy.

Why can't I want peace and paradise?

Like normal people?

"Makes you glad to be inside," Suki says, following his gaze out the window. "Doesn't it?"

"Yeah. You should spend the night. Please."

She takes a sip of her coffee, tempted but trying to sense if the timing is right, if it *feels* right. His eyes follow the cup as it goes to her lips and suddenly he notices the Starbucks logo turning toward him and the image comes at him like a close-up.

HAND OUT OF THE COCONUT

After she was arrested by Wyatt on the night he missed Howard at her trailer, Amber bailed out of jail and began court-ordered drug treatment through the Breaking the Cycle Program. BTC, as it is called, is run by the Pierce County Alliance, an efficient nonprofit organization that operates out of two buildings north of the courthouse. You can spot the buildings by the chain-smoking recovering addicts that congregate outside.

Because Amber is female and only an accomplice, the judge set her bail low enough that her mother could post it through C.J.'s Bail Bonds. She has mostly complied with the BTC program—lapsing twice—and hopes that eventually she can make a plea bargain with the prosecutor, so she can win back custody of her daughter.

Wyatt asked her to meet him at the Kickstand Café not just because it is close to the Alliance buildings, but because it is next door to his favorite movie house, the Grand Cinema. The Grand, a Tacoma icon, shows independent films in cozy and intimate spaces that put Wyatt in mind of a private screening room, though he has never been in one.

Suki wants to see an arty love story—Wyatt cannot remember the title—and so he scheduled this meeting to precede the movie, slipping in work before recreation, as is his wont.

Wyatt sits with his back to the west wall, facing the door, sipping a mocha. Used books line the shelves of the walls below black and white landscape photographs. Tattered copies of *The Stranger, The Volcano,* and other papers lie on the aluminum and glass tables. An old bicycle hangs on the south wall.

Amber enters wearing a ratty overcoat, and though Wyatt cannot see her body he can see her face and it is noticeably fuller and without scabs, her teeth look okay, and her eyes do not look dilated or haunted. He quickly decides she is off meth, maybe ready to pull her hand out of the coconut.

"Thanks for agreeing to meet with me," he says, standing to greet her and shaking her hand, which she receives awkwardly.

"Sure."

"You want some coffee or anything?"

"No," she says, sitting. "No, thank you."

Though there are three other customers in the room, two are a chatty couple and the third is typing away on his laptop, so Wyatt feels he and Amber have sufficient privacy.

They exchange small talk about the difficulties of recovery for a few minutes and she seems relatively calm, albeit down, another sign she is clean.

"I want to try PROMETA," Amber tells him.

"Yeah, I hear it's the new silver bullet."

While meth saps the brain's ability to generate dopamine, causing long-term tweekers to be hopelessly depressed when they are not high, PROMETA reportedly reboots their brains to eliminate the cravings and the depression, restoring them to a pre-meth state. Wyatt is thinking of investing in Hythiam, the company that owns the patent on the PROMETA program. Rush Limbaugh and Chris Farley's family are reportedly supporters.

"Friends tell me it works, like they don't even have the desire to use anymore," Amber says. "But they're still left with all the issues that made them do drugs in the first place."

"There's ongoing counseling for that."

"I know, that's why I want to get into the drug court PROMETA program, but they won't let in people with manufacturing charges."

"That's what I'm here to maybe help with."

"Yeah?"

Wyatt nods reassuringly.

"I want my child back," Amber blurts out.

"I understand. And I want Howard. So maybe we can work something out."

"You can help me get my child back?" Her eyes well up.

"I understand this is emotional for you, but I want to talk business, okay?"

"Okay." She holds back the tears, arms clutched across her chest, holding the overcoat tight over her thin body.

"You're facing manufacturing charges now?"

"Right."

"And Endangerment of a Child?"

"Right."

"So you're looking at seventy-five to ninety-two months in prison, unless we can get you into drug court."

"What about a DOSA?"

"You would still do some prison time with DOSA, though not much."

"Any time is too much. I can't get my child back if I'm in prison."

"I can talk to the prosecutor about drug court."

"You can get me in?"

"I can't guarantee anything."

"Who's the prosecutor in drug court? Rose? I hear she screams at the judge to not let in anyone with manufacturing charges."

"I'll talk to Mike Lawson, the chief of the drug trial unit, and he'll talk to Rose."

"So what do I have to do?"

"You ready to talk about Howard?"

Amber nods and proceeds to tell him all she knows, but by now he already suspects most of what she offers: Howard is expanding, he is involved in identity theft and other scams, he has a network of tweekers working for him, he is pissing off the bikers and the Mexicans, and he is living at Brandy's house near Eatonville and there is a large lab in the barn.

"I've heard about the barn, but I can't get a warrant unless I have info from someone reliable who has firsthand info."

"Firsthand?"

"Seen something themselves."

"I haven't."

"Who would have?"

"You checked with the midget?"

"Not yet. Does the midget have a name?"

"Clay, I think. But everyone just calls him the midget."

"Has he been in the barn?"

"I don't know, but maybe. I could ask around?"

Wyatt nods. "What about you?" He studies the eagerness to please in her face. "Could you get in there? Hook back up with him? Get him to talk about the lab?"

Amber slumps and sighs.

"He knows you," Wyatt says quietly. "He trusts you."

"He doesn't trust anyone. And he's smart. You don't realize how smart he is."

Tweekers, like domestic violence victims, usually have a perverse loyalty to their man. Wyatt recognizes that if not for the leverage of her child, she would not even talk to him, let alone set up Howard.

"I need you to get close to him again."

"That will mean using again."

"Not necessarily."

"I'll *have to* use to get back with him. If I don't, he'll be all suspicious. It's not like he doesn't know everyone is after him. And besides, I mean, you know, he doesn't spend time with girls who don't use. So . . . you'll tell my counselor it's okay that I'm using?"

This last line hits him and he leans back and contemplates the downside of this approach, frowning.

"I'll do it," she says, "I just want my child back." Tears begin. "I just want her back."

"This may not be the best plan. . . ."

"No, no," she says, "I'll do it, just tell me you'll get my child back. I know you can help." She uncrosses her arms, leans forward, reaches across the table. "I won't fuck up again, I promise, tell me what I have to do and I'll do it." As she sobs, the words spill together. "I just want her back."

"Okay, okay," he says, holding her offered hands on the table. "You've given me enough. I'll put in a word to the prosecutor."

"I'll do this if you want me to. I *will*. I can get back with him. Howard knew I wasn't just a bag 'ho, I was one of his favorites."

"I'm sorry," Wyatt says, wearing his cell phone headset as he drives south on I-5. Rain patters the roof and windshield and he cannot hear well, but well enough to pick up Suki's anger.

"I really wanted to see that movie."

"We can see the late show tonight."

"I have to open the shop tomorrow. And it opens at six a.m. Remember? Coffee junkies like to get started early."

"Later this week, then, the movie will still be there."

"That's not the point."

"Sorry, but I have this new lead I have to follow up on."

"Now? You have to follow up on it now?"

"Yes, sorry."

"We were supposed to see the movie right after your interview. Where are you?"

"I'm driving. Tweekers don't stay still long, and I know where this person is staying for the moment. I didn't want to get into it and then have to cancel on you at the last minute."

"You don't consider this the last minute?"

"Okay, good point."

"If Howard doesn't kill you, I will."

Wyatt laughs, hoping this will ease the tension.

"I'm not trying to be funny."

"I'll make it up to you." He shifts lanes into the far left, speeds up through the increasing rain. "I promise."

"I try to have faith in you, and then . . ."

"I'll make it up to you in a big way."

"I don't know, Wyatt. I really don't." Her anger segues into disappointment, which is more difficult for both of them to deal with. "I'll talk to you later."

"Hold on, Suki. How about if I call you after I check this out?"

He realizes at this point that the connection is lost—she hung up. He misses the definitiveness of the dial tone that followed a hang-up when people used land lines.

He turns on KJR, the same radio station he listened to as a kid. The playlist has not changed much. After a few songs he knows and likes, he drives slowly down a dirt road through a mobile home park. Thanks to the heavy rain, everybody is inside, including the children and animals that are usually darting around in front of cars.

He has been here before investigating child molestation, meth labs, and stolen property. The litter scattered all about—tires, broken televisions, abandoned toys—represents the mind-set of the inhabitants for him.

A blue tarp hangs over the front door of a double-wide mobile home at the end of the road. Wyatt parks close, parallel to a row of mismatched garbage cans. As he steps out of his car and toward the door he can feel eyes on him.

"Open up," he says after his second knock. "It's Detective Wyatt James."

Shaking his head impatiently, he listens to the customary scurrying back and forth and then the footsteps of someone coming to the door.

"Yes?" a tall and gaunt woman says, opening the flimsy trailer door.

"I need to talk to Clay."

"There's no Clay here."

"The midget."

"I'll check and see if he's here."

"You mean he could be here without you knowing it?"

"I . . . just got home."

Wyatt gently pushes her aside as he enters.

"Someone's here, Clay," she says. "It's a cop."

Clay steps out of a bathroom door and smiles at Wyatt as though he is thrilled to see him, hands held out to his side where the officer can see them.

"We need to talk," Wyatt says.

"Leave us," Clay says to the six-foot woman.

"We can talk out in my car if you would prefer," Wyatt says.

"No, here's fine." Clay jerks his thumb in the direction of the door and, to Wyatt's surprise, the tall woman picks up a jacket from the floor and heads out silently, closing the door behind her.

"Sit down," Clay offers, gesturing magnanimously at the couch, which is speckled with cat hair and stains of undeterminable origin.

Wyatt, not wanting to ruin his blue blazer or khakis and not wanting a long conversation, continues standing.

"No, thanks."

Clay hops up on the couch and sits. A disassembled computer lies in pieces on the coffee table, next to a copy of *Barely Legal* and several empty cans of Mountain Dew with cigarette butts on the rims.

"I heard you were shot," Clay says.

"Who did you hear that from?"

"Just one of those things you hear. Cops don't get shot that often."

"They seem to in Pierce County."

"I heard the guy who shot you is dead."

"Who did he work for?"

"Bikers."

"Howard?"

"Nope."

"When did you last see Howard?"

"It's been a while."

"When?"

Clay and Wyatt look at each other for a long beat, Clay trying to gauge how much he can lie to Wyatt and Wyatt trying to look like he knows more than he does so that Clay does not lie too much.

"This is off the record," Clay says. "Right?"

"Okay."

"He would kill me if he knew I told you anything. Even if I was lying to protect him. He'd kill me for just talking to you."

"Howard's never killed anyone before. Has he?"

"No, not that I know of, but he cut off a guy's hand recently. With a chainsaw. Howard's on a run, he's got meth bugs, and he's getting worse, much worse, crazy paranoid and . . . I don't know, I'm hearing about all sorts of weirdness."

"When did you see him?"

"And you won't tell my BTC counselor, either?"

"When did you start BTC?"

"Just a possession charge. No biggie. But I hate jail, so my counselor can't know I'm, you know, associating with dealers and users."

"Secrets are safe with me."

"And you can help me with the charges?"

"Don't push it, Clay. You're just facing possession charges. Save my help for when you really need it."

"Okay, I hear that."

"So when did you see him last?" When Clay hesitates, Wyatt adds, "This is just confidential background stuff."

"Confidential, double-secret?"

"Sure, double-secret probation."

"Three weeks ago."

"Where?"

"His house."

"His house? You were inside?"

"Yeah. I'm connected, I'm trusted. That's why this has to be double-secret whatever you said."

"Does he have a lab in there?"

"Not in the house. Not that I could see. I think it's in the barn out back."

"What makes you say that? Did you see anything?"

"No, I've just heard."

"He's living with a woman named Brandy."

"Teenager?"

"No, that's her daughter, Porsche. She's twelve."

"I thought she seemed kinda young to be his girlfriend."

"You see any signs of a lab?"

"No."

"Any drugs?"

"Meth."

"Did he sell it to you?"

Clay hesitates, looks down at his small feet dangling off the floor.

"How much did he sell you?" Wyatt continues.

"Just a quarter."

"Did he have more there?"

"I don't know, I assume so."

"Did you see any large quantities?"

"No."

"Did you see anything I should know about?"

"No."

"Guns?"

"Didn't see any."

Wyatt starts to head toward the door, but turns. He watches Clay twitch for a moment.

"Clay?"

"Yeah?"

"Nothing personal, but I'm going to have to tell your counselor to run a piss test on you."

"What? You said all of this was off the record. Double-secret confidential."

I had to tell you lies to help you get to the truth.

"You know I hate jail," Clay continues. "Those fuckers are all over me." He vaults off the couch, yells up at Wyatt, face at crotch level. "They use me for midget-tossing contests!"

Wyatt steps out into the rain. Clay's girlfriend is standing under the blue tarp, calmly smoking.

"Clay will have a UA next week at BTC," Wyatt says as he passes her. "If he's not clean, he'll go to jail. His choice."

Though she stares at him uncomprehending for a moment, exhaling a stream of nicotine into the cold air, Wyatt expects she will eventually understand.

"Not enough," Mike says, sipping his tom yum soup out of a large plastic spoon, savoring the tangy flavor and warmth. Outside, the air is chilly with the frisson of snow on the horizon.

"He knows he's got a lab in the barn," Wyatt insists, his Viet curry untouched.

Mike reaches for the Blue Willow teapot and fills their cups. "No, he doesn't *know*."

"Well, *I* know."

"And you're right, but being right isn't enough."

"The midget's reliable."

"I'm not sure the midget qualifies as reliable, and anyway, he doesn't have any fresh information." Mike has this same conversation repeatedly with officers who think, quite sensibly, that they ought to be able to get a warrant for a house if there is criminal activity inside, but it is not that simple. "You know the Aguilar-Spinelli test."

"Yeah, it requires a good informant."

"A *reliable* informant, one with personal knowledge that isn't stale."

"Yeah, I know."

"Well, you've got a questionable informant: half of his information is hearsay, and all of it's probably stale."

"You just keep raining on my parade, Counselor."

"That's what I'm here for. Eat, the food's excellent."

Mike comes to Le-Le's on Martin Luther King Jr. Way almost every day for lunch, and sometimes for dinner, since he does not cook. When he discovered the place it was a dive and he liked it that way. After more people heard about it and started coming, Le-Le and her husband painted a rice paddy mural on the walls, put the menus in plastic jackets, hung peasant hats from the ceiling, added bamboo plants, and raised the prices. Mike liked it better before it caught on, much as he liked his favorite bands such as the Replacements, R.E.M., and U2 before they caught on, but he still comes regularly.

"So what do you suggest?" Wyatt asks.

"Eat."

"Besides that," Wyatt says, having a bite.

"Nothing."

"Nothing? Are you getting Zen on me? I just want a warrant, not a fucking Zen lesson."

"Hello, Judge."

Mike confirms his attendance at an upcoming charity event the judge is supporting, and he promises the judge he will invite some lawyers and politicos she does not know how to reach but would like to see there.

"You know too many people," Wyatt says after the judge moves on, soliciting more lawyers as she works her way toward a corner table where a *News Tribune* reporter sips a bubble tea.

"People are interesting."

"Interesting is one way to put it."

Le-Le's reminds Mike of Rick's, Humphrey Bogart's café in *Casablanca*. Everybody comes to Le-Le's. Sometimes he can save himself half a dozen phone calls and e-mails by the time he leaves.

"You remember Bruce Lee?" Mike asks.

"Yes."

"A master."

"Yes."

"One of the best in the world at what he did?"

"Yes."

"Someone who understood the art of excellence?"

"Yes. Is this a cross-examination?"

"Someone we would be wise to emulate?"

"Except for the heart attack at a young age, yes."

"Well, here's what Bruce Lee had to say about your situation."

"*My* situation?"

"Your pursuit of Howard."

"Lee is speaking from his grave in Seattle?"

" 'The less effort you apply, the faster and more powerful you will be.' "

Wyatt nods, seeing the wisdom of this as it applies to punching someone, or even hitting a golf ball, but not convinced of its larger application to life.

"And you believe this?" Wyatt asks.

"Yes."

"Then why work so hard?"

"Remember when I was telling you I didn't quite get the whole Nirvana concept? If Nirvana is not wanting anything, then why want Nirvana?"

"I agreed."

"Right, and I eventually quit wanting Nirvana. And so it started coming to me. And I'd like it, and then want it too bad, and it would go away. And then I'd quit wanting it so bad, and it would come back." Mike shrugs. "Nirvana is like criminals and women that way. We catch what we're not chasing too hard."

"You trying to tell me to pull my hand out of the coconut?"

Mike sips his tea. "When you stop and connect with the world, possibilities open up."

"Suki came back," Wyatt says after a long pause.

"See?"

"But I think I fucked it up again."

"Well, no amount of Zen can stop men from screwing up relationships. Buddha bailed on his wife and son and stayed a bachelor for the rest of his weird life."

TO EVERYTHING THERE IS A SEASON

Thanksgiving passes; Christmas approaches.

Mike reaches over and turns up the defroster and then the CD player, clicking on Death Cab for Cutie. He quickly refocuses on the road as the Range Rover slides in its lane. Snowflakes fall gently toward the windshield and then suddenly whoosh away in the air flow around the car.

He drives past the Bullseye Shooting Range and the Bubble Room, a bar where he used to drink after work when he and his colleagues were younger and had more time and energy and questions to discuss. Green and red lights blink around the windows.

"Stop for a cocktail, or continue on?"

"Continue on," Wyatt says. "Poker awaits us."

"The holy game of poker."

"Good for the soul."

"What's the difference between a poker room and a church?"

"Is this a joke?"

"When you pray in a poker room, you really mean it."

Ahead the road is nearly empty and the snow is falling fast enough that the pavement is covered in white. On a night like this Mike would not normally be driving. When the snow started, he was staring out at the rock garden from the kitchen where he was sitting on a stool, spacing out. After the snow started sticking, he felt compelled to venture outside.

"I keep reading these articles about how we should fight terrorism more like crime and less like a war," Wyatt says, "but I don't know about that. People would be pissed if we caught

Osama bin Laden and had to let him walk because it was a pretextual stop or there was a technical defect in a search warrant."

"You're still thinking about Howard."

"Only tangentially. You think criminals and terrorists are similar?"

"There will always be bad guys, and there will always be evil, so I guess crime and terrorism are similar in that the battle is endless, so we have permanent job security."

"Would you rather convert to Islam, or have your head chopped off?"

"The Islamic fascists hate rock and roll, so they will never prevail." Mike turns up Death Cab for Cutie. "Always bet on the good guys in the long run."

"Cool CD," Wyatt says. "Suki's into it. Glad to see you're keeping up with the kids."

"They used to play on the local scene. Pete Tyler introduced me to their Barsuk albums, and I've followed their career through the years."

Mike slows down as the snow increases, flakes swarming over the front window. Ahead of them a neon sign beckons, FREDDIE'S, shining in red cursive.

"Best poker movie?" Wyatt asks. "*Cincinnati Kid,* or *Rounders*?"

"Close call," Mike says, pleased that Wyatt is letting Howard go, if only for the moment, "but I have to say *Rounders*."

"Best line in *Rounders*?"

"'If you're too careful, your whole life can become a fucking grind.'"

"'We can't run from who we are. Our destiny chooses us.'"

"The line about the blow job from Christy Turlington was pretty good, too, but I can't remember it exactly."

Mike pulls the Rover up into the mostly empty parking lot beside a dark rape van. The snow crunches when he steps out. Crossing in front of the Rover, he sees a Starbucks cup on the ground and, before Wyatt can notice, he kicks it under the car.

Just before they arrive at the glass doors of the casino, Wyatt's phone rings. He checks the LCD display, recognizes the number as one of his crew.

"Let it go," Mike says, sensing the call has something to do with Howard. "At least for tonight."

Wyatt flips open the phone. "Yeah?"

"Just received a report of shots fired out at Howard's lab," the hyped deputy says. "Sounds like they've got a fucking shoot-out going on, craziness, massive calls coming in. What do you think?"

"How far from the scene are you?"

"Twenty minutes, maybe."

"I'll be behind you, coming in a gray Range Rover. Don't shoot my ass."

"Roger that."

Wyatt flicks the phone shut.

"Howard," Mike says, picking up on the adrenaline vibe.

"Let's put your SUV to use."

THE SNOWS OF MOUNT RAINIER

Gunshots crack in the cold air from different directions, the echoes muffled by the trees and snow covering the surrounding hills.

Two bikers are shooting at Brandy's house from inside the barn, poking their semiautomatic AR-15 rifles with long hundred-round magazines around the doors. Orange and yellow flashes cut through the darkness. Toxic fumes from leaking anhydrous ammonia tanks cause their eyes to water and disrupt their aim.

One biker is shooting from the creek bank, the bare trees providing little cover. He is crouched down with a .50 Beowulf, a powerful variation on the AR-15, and he has a good angle on a back corner of the house and is more sparing with his shots than his friends in the barn who smoked meth just before they raided Howard's lab.

All of the bikers are using .223 hollow-point bullets, which shatter an entire window on impact and slam into the house with a scary *whap*, but do not fully penetrate walls. They came to destroy Howard's lab, which they have done. Only after he started shooting at them from the house did they decide to kill him.

Howard and Brandy fire back from shattered windows in the kitchen, recklessly triggering off shots in the general direction of the barn. They are using target ammunition and extra-long thirty-three-round magazines Howard bought on the Internet. Howard is wearing cargo pants and a T-shirt that reads JUST SAY NO TO BUGS in red letters over the black image of a cockroach lying dead on its back with a meth pipe in its mouth.

Flickering gray light from the television monitors connected to security cameras pulse in the dark kitchen, but the small and shadowy images on the screen only tell Howard what he already knows: people in the barn are shooting at him.

Though Howard went many years without owning guns because Washington State adds three years of prison for each gun if you are convicted of manufacturing methamphetamine, paranoia finally got the best of him and he bought the 9mm Glocks and now he feels his paranoia was justified.

Just because you're paranoid doesn't mean people aren't out to get you.

He purchased the guns through ads in the newspaper: cash for guns, no paperwork, no problems.

Porsche and Joe are in the living room, lying on the floor by the couch as ordered. Above them is a fresh Christmas tree, a Noble fir cut down from a neighbor's property, which is undecorated except for a zigzagging string of miniature white lights that twinkle in the dark room. Joe cannot stay still and Porsche keeps telling him he's a fool and to keep his head down.

"I wanna gun," Joe says as the shots continue.

"Fucking losers," Porsche says, face on the shag rug, not quite understanding why her life is like this, but certain it is the fault of men, *losers.*

Neighbors, not entirely unaccustomed to gunshots, are still stunned by the duration of the firefight and hide in protected corners of their houses, complaining to each other about high taxes and the lack of police in their rural community.

Howard, shooting through the shattered window at random intervals, feels at a disadvantage because the bikers have rifles and distance. He is particularly aggravated by the third biker sniping at him from the creek bank.

Brandy is on her knees at his feet reloading the Glock magazines, not thinking but just doing as she was told.

"Go into Porsche's bedroom," Howard says, "and look for the guy by the creek. Shoot him. I'm going to run for the barn."

"*What?*"

"We're sitting fucking ducks here, I'm going after the assholes in the barn."

"No, no, we're best off staying in!"

"Listen!" Howard yells. "You go into the bedroom and cover me when the fucker by the creek shoots. Now!"

Brandy scrambles off on her knees, fully loaded Glock in hand. In the hallway she jumps onto her feet and runs in a crouch, not slowing down to check on Porsche or Joe.

As Howard loads his magazine, the occasional AR-15 round flying over his head into the kitchen cabinets, Joe enters the kitchen carrying a .44 Magnum.

"Stay the fuck down," Howard yells.

Joe goes down, but still makes his way over, crawling like a soldier. Howard laughs at the sight of the small boy with the big gun.

"Where the fuck did you get that?"

"Mom's bedroom."

Howard recognizes it as the gun that was pointed at him the night he arrived. "Give it to me."

Joe pouts as he hands over the gun, the barrel carelessly pointed at Howard's stomach.

"Fucking kids," Howard says, spinning the chamber, confirming it is loaded.

"Am I supposed to just hide until I get shot?"

"You're supposed to do what you're fucking told." Though

Howard is twitching like crazy, he feels in control and focused from the lines he snorted. In retrospect he should have snuck up on the bikers, but he was so pissed—*fucking criminal trespassers*—he just broke out his meth and his gun and took care of business. "Can you fucking do that?" he asks Joe. "Can you fucking do what you're told?"

"Yeah," Joe says.

"Okay, that's a good kid." Howard hands Joe a loaded Glock, butt out into his small hand. Joe beams, lifting it, noticing the lightness compared to the .44 Magnum. "Remember, Joe, when I told you I thought you were a tough kid? And someday you'd have a chance to prove it?"

"Yeah?"

"Here's your chance. Once-in-a-lifetime, son. Once-in-a-fucking-lifetime."

Joe nods, enjoying the gun in his hand.

"I'm going to rush the barn," Howard says. "As I run out the back door, you stand up and start shooting at the front door of the barn. There's a couple bikers with rifles you're trying to hit. Shoot for their fat fucking bellies, okay?"

"Okay."

"You've shot-guns in those idiot video games, right?"

"Yeah?"

"Same idea, but the gun is going to kick back. You know what kick is? The gun is going to want to kick back toward you." Howard demonstrates with the Magnum, employing a two-handed police-style grip. "Just keep your elbows bent and let it come back a little, but not too much. Got it?"

"Got it."

"Good kid. Welcome to the real world."

With this, Howard scoots over to the back door and perches on his haunches. He shoves the Magnum into his waistband, takes a vial out of his jeans pocket, taps half of the unchopped white crystals onto the back of his hand, and sniffs it off in a swoop.

Harsh.

"Okay," he says, wiggling his nose. "Cover me."

Swinging open the door, he runs out into the backyard, barefoot, Magnum blazing in the direction of the barn. He almost instantly trips onto his face and drops the .44 as a bullet burns through a calf.

Brandy sees the flash of the shot from the dark of the creek bank and wildly shoots in that direction. Hearing the shots whizzing and hitting around him, the biker starts to slip back down the bank toward the icy water, but one of the bullets catches his arm and tears clean through and into his side.

As Joe hears the shots ringing out, he stands with the Glock in both hands and begins shooting at the opening of the barn as instructed. He does not see anybody, but suddenly there are white and orange flashes and the cabinets behind him splinter and he realizes *someone is shooting back.*

With Joe covering him, Howard crawls quickly back into the house, leaving the .44 behind. He shuts the door behind him after dragging his leg out of the way.

"Those pieces of shit shot me!"

Joe ducks down to join Howard and is shocked as he watches Howard pull his pant leg up and exposes a hole in his upper calf with blood pumping out in spurts and running down his boot.

"Get me a goddamn towel!"

After a moment more of staring at the wound, Joe grabs a

dirty dish towel from on the stove. He hands it to Howard, who loops it around his leg and ties a fast knot, which quickly turns red as the blood spreads like a blossom.

"You okay?" Brandy yells from the bedroom during a respite in shooting.

"Fucking great," Howard yells back.

"Is it over?" Porsche yells.

"Far fucking from it," Howard yells.

Sirens fade in as two fully marked Jeep Cherokees from the Pierce County Sheriff's Department pull up and stop on the road in front of Brandy's house, spaced out so one is thirty yards east of Brandy's driveway and the other is about thirty yards behind, their wig-wag lights shining on the snow, headlights on.

One of the security cameras is focused on the front of the house, a wide-angle shot, and Howard watches the arrival of the officers with mixed feelings. His chances of survival just went up, but his chance of escape just went down.

"Things are getting complicated," he says to Joe.

Two officers from each Jeep empty out of the driver's side onto the street, keeping the vehicles between themselves and the barn where the gunfire is reportedly centered.

"Sheriff's Department," Deputy Newton announces through his PA system. "Put your weapons down and come out with your hands on top of your head."

Though Newton is not sure where exactly the shooters will be coming out from—the barn or the house or the field that stretches to the creek—he thinks it best to initially address the situation with the traditional approach.

Seconds later there are several rapid-fire flashes and bangs from the barn and three of the four patrol car headlights explode and one wig-wag light goes dark. Suddenly a firefight is on as the deputies open up from behind their vehicles with shotguns and Glock .40s. The barn, at fifty yards, is at the limit of the range for the buckshot-loaded shotguns, but distance is hard to gauge in the dark and the snow.

Sensing an opportunity, Howard stands with a freshly loaded Glock and triggers off several rounds toward the door of the barn where he can see flashes from the bikers' guns.

"Yeah!" he yells, dropping back down. "I think I got one of the fuckers!"

Joe cheers and thrusts his fists in the air.

Brandy peers over the top of the bedroom window, staring at the spot where the biker was shooting from earlier, seeing no movement. Below her sight line the biker is lying in the shallow of the flowing creek, shivering and bleeding out, losing consciousness from a lucky shot.

Mike and Wyatt approach the scene as the gunfire subsides again, Wyatt on the cell phone alerting the deputies to their arrival. Mike turns off his headlights and slows down.

"Drop me here," Wyatt says, "and turn around."

Mike has always found police work fascinating, more visceral than the formalized battle of the courtroom, and he drives Wyatt all the way up to the rear of Deputy Newton's Jeep.

"Okay," Wyatt says, "leave me here and pull back."

Suddenly shots ring out, distinctly different guns firing, and Mike and Wyatt both duck, their heads almost meeting at the center console.

"Actually," Mike says, after another exchange between the barn and the house stops, "I think I'll just stay here."

"I don't want you to get shot, Counselor."

"Hey, you're the one who always gets shot."

"Once is not always."

"You spend any more time in the hospital, I'm going to ask Suki out."

"She doesn't like lawyers."

"As far as you know."

Wyatt, not having time to banter further, checks his Glock, confirms the fifteen-round magazine is fully loaded, then quickly exits the Rover. Hunched over, he jogs a few steps across the snow-covered road to Newton's Jeep, sliding in between the deputies who are hunched down by the tires.

"What's the story?" he asks.

"I don't know. We've got a couple shooters in the barn, and apparently people in the house are returning fire."

"Howard's probably in the house. There's a lab in the barn."

Newton smiles. "Howard? You think anyone else is in the house with him?" He looks up over the hood of the Jeep.

"Could be. Woman who owns the house has two kids."

"Shit. Let's give them another chance to come out."

Once again he picks up the handset from the PA system and announces, "Put down your weapons and come out with your hands up. Now."

"The 'now' should make all the difference," his partner says, then turns to Wyatt. "Last time we tried that they shot up the car and knocked out the lights."

"We may have taken them out," Newton says. "We shot off about fifty rounds."

"Let's wait until we have backup before we try to confirm that."

"Where the fuck *is* the backup?" Wyatt asks.

"Come on, we're too understaffed to keep officers out here. This is cook territory."

"With the snow and ice," Newton says, looking up at the large flakes continuing to fall, "I'm figuring we're on our own for a while."

Slowly lifting his head, Mike surveys the scene, noting that the deputies are positioned behind the wheels of their Jeeps. He opens his driver's door and steps out behind the large front tire of the Range Rover, crouching and poking his head over the hood.

"Hey," Wyatt whispers, gesturing for Mike to keep his head down.

Mike does, turning and sitting. Just next to him is a pothole. He stares at the icy water in the pothole for a moment, watching the snowflakes dissolve on contact. The shadows of their crystal pattern linger for a split second on the surface, the amazing symmetry lingering in his mind.

The blissful sensation he hoped to recapture with the birdbath suddenly comes to him, rising from his chilly feet and through his body and into his head, and once again, for the second time in his life, he truly understands that everything is ordered, everything is connected, everything is cool.

"What the fuck are you doing out here?" Wyatt whispers, snapping Mike out of his bliss.

"Taking cover."

"Fucking lawyers." Wyatt shakes his head at the deputies. "Is anyone watching the back to cut off Howard's escape?"

"Yeah, whoever was shooting from the barn."

"Rival dealers?"

"I assume so."

"I gotta think Howard would rather give up to us than be shot by them," the other deputy says.

"I don't know," Wyatt says.

In the bedroom Brandy replaces the dish towel around Howard's leg with a clean white T-shirt, which turns red even quicker than the towel. He takes three Vicodins from his pocket and chews them down while she tightens a second T-shirt around the wound.

"Where's Porsche?" Howard asks.

"Hiding by the couch in the living room," Joe says, reloading Howard's Glocks.

"Get in here, Porsche," Howard yells.

"No!"

"Where are the car keys?" Howard asks Brandy.

"In my purse."

"Give them to me."

Brandy quickly pulls the keys out of her purse and hands them to Howard, confused but not really wanting clarification.

"Get back here, Porsche," Howard yells again.

"No!"

"Do I have to drag you back here?"

"No!"

Howard turns to Brandy. "What's that mean?"

"She's not moving."

"Shit. Okay. We'll go out there. Stay down."

Howard takes his two reloaded Glocks from Joe and starts snaking along on his stomach to the living room. Brandy and Joe follow, crawling. Their Christmas tree lights are flickering and a soft light from the whiteness outside filters through the mini blinds, closed as always since Howard came to stay.

Porsche is crying softly on the floor.

"I'm going to miss you, hon," Howard says.

Porsche scowls back at him, noticing fresh scabs on his fore-head, just like her mother has acquired of late. Brandy, reacting to the revulsion on Porsche's face, crawls over and hugs her awkwardly on the floor.

"I'm sorry," she whispers.

Howard, sitting up beside them, admires the bright tattoo around Porsche's ankle, a bracelet of roses and thorns with drops of blood, *something to remember me by*.

"I'm looking at ten years if I surrender," he says, shoving the Glocks into his waistband and lighting up what he imagines could be his last cigarette. "And Howard Schultz isn't really the type to surrender."

"Well, you're not really Howard Schultz," Brandy says back, surprising herself.

Vaguely registering an insurrection, Howard takes a long drag of his Kool, drops the butt onto the floor. He climbs up onto one knee and uses his good leg to push himself up onto his feet.

From out of his pocket he pulls a meth pipe, which he ceremoniously slides onto the tip of the Christmas tree.

"Bo-orn is the ki-ing of methlehem," he sings.

"What are you doing?" Brandy asks.

He looks at her. *She'll always have those sad cow eyes.* "I'm going to Ireland," he says, stepping unsteadily toward the front door, pulling a Glock out of his waistband. "They don't extradite."

Brandy puts an arm around each child and brings them under her and covers them up as much as she can, shaking, anticipating the worst. As has happened many times before, it occurs to her that her latest boyfriend is borderline psychotic and a menace and no good for her or her children. She tells herself she cannot keep making the same mistake, as she has told herself so many times before.

"Wish me luck," Howard says.

"What-fucking-ever," Porsche mutters.

Howard, limping into the entry hall, does not hear. "You out there, Wyatt," he yells at the closed front door, then opens it a crack. "Come on, Wyatt. Don't disappoint me."

Hearing the voice, Wyatt and the deputies rise slightly, level their guns toward the half-open door. Mike turns and gets up on his knees, peers over the hood.

"Shit," Newton says, "is he coming out?"

"Yeah, I'm here, Howard," Wyatt yells back.

"The king is dead," Howard yells. "Long live the king. Right, Wyatt?"

"He's tweaking big time," Newton says.

"You know the drill, Howard." Wyatt stands, gun held out with both hands. "Come out with your hands up."

"Don't fucking bet on it."

Howard pulls out the vial, taps the remaining contents onto the side of the Glock barrel. He drops the vial, breathes in deeply, exhales, then sniffs up the last of the meth off the barrel, blinking and contorting his face as the crystals burn into his nostrils.

Most of his dopamine neurotransmitters have been destroyed, and his brain resembles that of a Parkinson's patient, but there are still enough neurons left for him to feel a bit of the old chemical zoom. He begins humming, *I am Superman, and I can do any-thing . . .*

After wiping his dripping nose, Howard pulls the second Glock out of his pants and flings the door open and runs out across the snow-covered yard toward Brandy's car, guns in hand. At first nobody shoots, Wyatt and the deputies frozen by the sudden and audacious sprint, but then Howard points his guns toward Wyatt and the patrol cars.

Nearly simultaneously they all get off shots, two of the officers with shotguns, and Howard takes several rounds of buckshot and three .40-caliber rounds—two hollow-point slugs ripping into his chest—and he writhes and stumbles, but he keeps firing his guns as he falls.

Mike stares as the muzzle blasts flare in the darkness and momentarily light up the scene in still frames. He is thinking he should duck, but he cannot pull his eyes away. Howard triggers off one last shot and Mike sees the flash just as the bullet pierces his forehead.

"The Bible assures us love is stronger even than death." The priest's amplified voice echoes through the dark building and resonates off the giant stained-glass image of Jesus bleeding on the cross and glowing in the light from outside.

Police and prosecutors in dark suits fill the gallery and tears flow from some, but not from Wyatt. Suki, to his left, was emotional the night before but is calm now, facing forward.

"For God so loved the world that he gave his only Son, so that everyone who believes in Him will not perish but have eternal life. God did not send His Son into the world to condemn it, but to save it."

This is only the second time Wyatt has been in a church in the last ten years and as the priest continues to tie together death and love with the ponderous tone of a Russian novelist, Wyatt's mind hopscotches through subjects, including the Holy Ghost, which he is still not clear on, and Mike and the incomprehensible void of death.

Wyatt has always been contemptuous of those who chase money or power or drugs, simultaneously recognizing that we especially dislike in others those qualities that we dislike in ourselves. His own taste for the chase, he has always told himself, is *different*. This rationalization, however, popped like a party balloon upon Mike's death.

Chasing something, no matter our target, can be one of many ways to avoid absorbing and appreciating the details of our passing lives, to avoid facing the only issue that matters, the scariest and surest issue, death. Mike was trying to tell him this, to slow down and connect to the possibilities, but of course Mike often handed out advice, usually based on his own evolving code of conduct, and Wyatt enjoyed the conversations but did not pay Mike's counsel much heed.

There are not many advantages to being dead, but one is that people think back on what you said and give it more weight than they ever did when you were alive.

Mike seemed to know that his destiny was an early death and this, to Wyatt, suggests the death was not senseless. He clings to this belief despite a lack of proof—*it has a reason even if I don't know it.*

Very Zen, Mike might say.

Mike would, Wyatt feels, be glad to see so many wearing his preferred uniform of dark suits and white shirts.

"Could you please face each other?" the priest asks.

Wyatt pivots on the altar. Suki's veil is open around her face and though Wyatt knows marriage is about much more than physical attraction, her beauty alleviates his anxiety.

Beauty is a miracle drug.

"Will you, Wyatt Evans James, take Suki Rebecca Kubomoto to be your lawfully wedded wife?"

"I will."

Wyatt slips into the moment as the priest repeats the litany to Suki and they exchange rings, "an endless circle," and then hold each other's hands, their arms stretched between them in a V.

"Let us now bow our heads and pray together. Dear Father, in sending us your only Son, Jesus Christ the Savior, You showed us that love must be carnate."

Had to tell you lies to help you get to the truth.

"Love is not just a thought, love is flesh, love is action. We humbly ask You now to nurture with Your love the love of Wyatt and Suki so that their love may be nurtured in others. Amen."

"Amen," responds the crowd, not quite in unison.

Wyatt did not want a church wedding and his friends and colleagues did not expect a church wedding, but Suki's mother did and so here they are.

"Before this community of supporters, according to the laws of Washington and the ordinance of God, I now pronounce you husband and wife. May God's joy, a joy this world cannot give and cannot take away, be with you forever. To signify this, you now may kiss."

They do and then turn to face the applause and a few hollers from his crew. Wyatt wanted either "I Will Dare" by the Replacements, or "I'm Not Down" by the Clash to fade in at this point, but Suki wanted "Yellow" by Coldplay or "Caring Is Creepy" by the Shins, and the latter was unacceptable to Wyatt because the Shins sold a song to McDonald's and the former was just unacceptable. They compromised on Morphine's "Cure for Pain," which plays as they step down the aisle, smiling as the cameras flash and seal their images in memory chips.

MAHALO

Hawaii's longest reef stretches out parallel to Anini Beach on the island of Kauai over a hundred yards out from the khaki-colored sand. Rolling waves break over the reef in a continually rushing white froth while the bay remains calm, the azure surface stirring only slightly, the bright morning sun glittering hypnotically off the ripples.

This, Wyatt thinks, *is solid evidence of the Holy Ghost.*

"If we evolved from monkeys," Suki asks, looking up a palm tree, "how come monkeys are still around?"

Wyatt looks at her out of the corner of his eye.

"I don't want to ever leave here," Suki says.

Wyatt cannot argue.

"I'm glad tourist season doesn't mean that you can shoot tourists."

Again, Wyatt cannot argue.

They sit on white beach chairs only a few yards in front of their vacation rental house, drinking Coronas with lime, gazing out at the water through sunglasses, paperbacks in the sand beside them.

Suki is wearing a new white-and-beige-striped bikini and much suntan lotion. Wyatt, wearing khaki shorts and a white aloha shirt, is almost color-coordinated. This is not intentional.

"How am I just discovering this place at forty?"

"I can answer that."

"Yeah?"

"Me."

He nods, sips his beer.

"Don't need much in a place like this," she says. "Don't need much at all."

"Cold beer is good." He holds the bottle up toward the sun, studies the light diffusing through the glass. "Sometimes I feel like everything in life takes too long. We learn things too late."

"Not too late. We learn when we learn."

Yet again he cannot argue. It does not seem right to quibble in the midst of so much beauty.

In the palm trees and lush foliage behind them colorful birds flap and caw and chirp. Their sounds are unlike birds in the Northwest, louder and sharper. Wyatt's senses suddenly heighten.

An airliner streaks across the clear blue sky, ascending, and as Wyatt's gaze shifts up he sees a gray feather drifting toward him. He watches it flutter, smiles after a moment.

Mahalo.

ABOUT THE AUTHOR

Mark Lindquist is the author of several acclaimed novels, including *Never Mind Nirvana*. His books have been published in eight languages. He has written screenplays, and articles for the *Los Angeles Times Book Review*, *New York Times Book Review*, the *Seattle Times*, *Details*, *The New York Times Sunday Magazine*, *Movieline*, and other publications. In 1995 Lindquist became a prosecuting attorney, and in 2004 he became the trial team chief of the drug unit for the prosecuting attorney in Pierce County. He lives in Tacoma. www.MarkLinquist.net

THE CHANUKKAH GUEST

THE CHANUKKAH GUEST

Eric A. Kimmel

illustrated by
Giora Carmi

Holiday House/New York

Bubba —"Grandmother" or "Granny."

dreidel — a four-sided top. The letters on each of the four sides stand for Hebrew words meaning, "A Great Miracle Happened There."

latke — a potato pancake, usually eaten with applesauce, jam, or sour cream.

menorah—"candlestick." The Chanukkah menorah has holders for nine candles, eight for each of the eight days of Chanukkah, and an additional one for the "shammes" or "servant" candle which is used to light the others.

This story first appeared in
Cricket, the Magazine for Children

Text copyright © 1988 by Eric A. Kimmel
Illustrations copyright © 1990 by Giora Carmi
All rights reserved
Printed in the United States of America

Library of Congress Cataloging-in-Publication Data
Kimmel, Eric A.
    The Chanukkah guest / written by Eric A. Kimmel ; illustrated
by Giora Carmi.
        p.   cm.
    Summary: On the first night of Chanukkah, Old Bear wanders
into Bubba Brayna's house and receives a delicious helping of
potato latkes when she mistakes him for the rabbi.
    ISBN 0-8234-0788-8
    [1. Hanukkah—Fiction. 2. Bears—Fiction.] I. Carmi, Giora,
ill. II. Title.
PZ7.K5648Cg 1990 [E]—dc20   89-20073 CIP
    ISBN 0-8234-0978-3 (pbk.)

For Aunt Florence and Aunt Ann

E.A.K.

To my family, who bears with me

G.C.

Old Bear roused himself from his winter sleep. He yawned a gigantic yawn. Then he stretched himself all over. Finally he poked his nose outside his den. A soft blanket of deep snow covered the ground. Spring was still many months away. Old Bear wrinkled his nose. What was that delicious smell? It smelled like something to eat, which reminded Old Bear that it had been months since he had eaten anything. Old Bear's empty stomach rumbled. He shook himself all over, then lumbered out of his den to follow the delicious smell.

Bubba Brayna took the last potato latke from the pan and put it in the oven with the others. The latkes would stay warm in there until her guests arrived. Bubba Brayna was ninety-seven years old and did not hear or see as well as she used to, but she still made the best potato latkes in the village. Every year at Chanukkah time all her friends made their way through the snow to her little house on the edge of the forest. How they loved those latkes! Bubba Brayna always made plenty. But tonight, on the first night of Chanukkah, she made twice as many as usual. Tonight was special. Tonight the rabbi was coming.

Bubba Brayna put on a clean apron and set the table. She filled a bowl with nuts for the dreidel game. Kitzel the cat rubbed against her ankles as she bustled around the kitchen. One last chore: the candles for the menorah. Bubba Brayna went to get them. Just then she heard a knock at the door.

It wasn't exactly a knock; more like a soft thumping. "My guests must be early," Bubba Brayna said. She opened the door. The cat hissed and dived under the table.

"Why, Rabbi, how nice to see you!" Bubba Brayna exclaimed.

"Grrrumph," growled Old Bear.

"And Happy Chanukkah to you, too. Please come in."

Old Bear lumbered into the house. He shook the snow from his fur.

"I'll take your coat, Rabbi. My, how thick it is! It must be very cold outside." Bubba Brayna tugged at Old Bear's fur.

"Grrrrrowwww!" Old Bear roared.

"Oh, you prefer to leave your coat on? Well, that's all right. It is a bit chilly in here. Come into the kitchen. I've set the table for a lovely Chanukkah evening."

Old Bear followed Bubba Brayna into the kitchen. The delicious smells made his nose twitch.

"Rrrrrumph!"

"Thank you, Rabbi. How kind of you to say that. The latkes will taste even better than they smell."

Old Bear followed his nose to the oven.

"RRROOOOWRGH!"

"Rabbi, I'm surprised at you! You know we don't eat until we light the menorah."

"Grrrrrr!"

"That's all right. I know you were teasing. I'll light the candles. Will you say the blessings?"

"Rrrumph."

Bubba Brayna struck a match and lit the shammes candle. Then she lit the one for the first night. Old Bear muttered and growled.

"Rrrumph . . . grrroooowr . . . rrrrr . . ."

" '. . . who has kept us, preserved us, and sustained us to this time.' Oh, Rabbi, you say the blessings so beautifully!"

Bubba Brayna pulled out a chair. Old Bear sat down.

"Let's play dreidel. I have some nuts we can play with."

Old Bear's nose twitched. He cracked a nut in his teeth.

"Rabbi, you won't have any nuts for the game if you eat them all."

"Rrrummmr," growled Old Bear.

"Don't worry. I have more nuts if you need them." Bubba Brayna gave the dreidel a spin. Old Bear sniffed at the little top as it whirled around. It stopped on the letter 'nun.'

"Nothing. We spin again." Bubba Brayna spun the dreidel once more. This time it stopped on the letter 'gimel.'

"I win!" Bubba Brayna swept the nuts into her apron.

"RRRROWRRRR!" Old Bear roared.

"Don't be angry, Rabbi. It's only a game. Here!" She tossed him a nut. Old Bear caught it in his paws, cracked it handily, then begged for more.

"No Rabbi, no more nuts. It's time for dinner."

Old Bear snuffled and grumbled. Bubba Brayna opened the oven door and took out a platter piled high with steaming potato latkes. Old Bear's nose twitched as she set them on the table. "Do you prefer your latkes with sour cream or jam?"

"Rrrrughrrr!" Old Bear growled.

"Jam. I thought so." Bubba Brayna smeared five big latkes with jam and stacked them on Old Bear's plate. Old Bear snuffled with pleasure as he gobbled the latkes down.

Bubba Brayna laughed. "You should use a fork. You have jam all over your beard." She wet a towel and wiped Old Bear's face. "I must tell you, Rabbi. You eat just like a bear."

"GRRROARRRURRRR!!!"
" 'I'm hungry as a bear, so I eat like one.' I can see that!" Bubba Brayna chuckled.

Old Bear ate and ate until all the latkes were gone. He licked jam and sour cream from his muzzle and his paws. Then Old Bear began to feel drowsy. He yawned. His great head flopped on Bubba Brayna's lap.

"Rabbi, you're sleepy. Who wouldn't be after such a meal? All the latkes are gone. It's time to go home. But before you leave I have a Chanukkah present for you." Bubba Brayna took out a red woolen scarf from the cupboard. She wrapped it around Old Bear's neck. "This scarf will keep you warm on the coldest nights. I knitted it myself."

"Grrrurrrrr." Old Bear licked Bubba Brayna's face.

Bubba Brayna blushed. "Oh, Rabbi! At my age!"

Old Bear shuffled to the door. It was time to return to his den. He felt very sleepy. "Rrrrumph," he growled as he ambled off into the night. He turned around one more time before disappearing into the forest. "Rrrrumph."

"Good night to you, too, Rabbi! Happy Chanukkah!"

Bubba Brayna was washing the dishes when she heard another knock. "I wonder who that is?"

"Shalom, Bubba Brayna!" Her friends and neighbors stood at the door wishing her a happy Chanukkah.

"Shalom, everybody!" Bubba Brayna cried. "How nice to see you. Please come in. I'm sorry I don't have any more latkes. The rabbi came by. He ate them all."

"Bubba Brayna, don't you recognize me?" It was the rabbi.

"The rabbi couldn't have eaten the latkes," everyone said. "He was in the synagogue with us the whole time."

Bubba Brayna scratched her head in bewilderment. "Something strange is happening here. Rabbi, I think there is an imposter going around. He looks like you. He talks like you. He even has your beard."

Just then Esther and David, Bubba Brayna's two grand-children, cried, "Come look!" Everyone ran to the kitchen to see what was wrong. They found the floor covered with bear tracks.

"A bear! And I thought it was the rabbi." Bubba Brayna had to sit down. Soon she began to giggle. "That was a very clever bear . . . or a very foolish Bubba Brayna. Ah well, let the bear have a happy Chanukkah. I had a happy Chanukkah too. And so will you, my dear friends.

David, go bring some potatoes up from the cellar. Esther, get my grater and bowl. Everybody has to help. You too, Rabbi. But I promise there will soon be latkes for everyone!"

Deep in the forest Old Bear slumbered in his den. His stomach was full of potato latkes. The warm woolen scarf was wrapped snugly around his neck.

Pleasant dreams, Old Bear. And Happy Chanukkah.